ON THE RUN

THE FUGITIVE FACTOR

GORDON KORMAN TAKES YOU TO THE EDGE OF ADVENTURE

ON THE RUN

BOOK ONE: CHASING THE FALCONERS

BOOK TWO: THE FUGITIVE FACTOR

DIVE

BOOK ONE: THE DISCOVERY

BOOK TWO: THE DEEP

BOOK THREE: THE DANGER

EVEREST

BOOK ONE: THE CONTEST

BOOK TWO: THE CLIMB

BOOK THREE: THE SUMMIT

ISLAND

BOOK ONE: SHIPWRECK

BOOK TWO: SURVIVAL

BOOK THREE: ESCAPE

www.SCHOLASTIC.com

www.GORDONKORMAN.com

GORDON KORMAN

ON THE RUN

CHASE #2

THE FUGITIVE FACTOR

AN
APPLE
PAPERBACK

SCHOLASTIC INC.

New York Toronto London Auckland Sydney
Mexico City New Delhi Hong Kong Buenos Aires

No part of this publication may be reproduced, or stored in a retrieval system, or transmitted in any form or by any means, electronic, mechanical, photocopying, recording, or otherwise, without written permission of the publisher. For information regarding permission, write to Scholastic Inc., Attention: Permissions Department, 557 Broadway, New York, NY 10012.

ISBN 0-439-65137-9

12 11 10 9 8 7 6 5 4 3   5 6 7 8 9 10/0

Printed in the U.S.A.   40

First printing, June 2005

ON THE RUN

THE FUGITIVE FACTOR

FALCONER KIDS STILL
AT LARGE

BURLINGTON, VT, AMALGA-MATED WIRE SERVICE: Aiden and Margaret Falconer, children of convicted traitors Drs. John and Louise Falconer, are the last two escapees still at large after the most daring prison break in the history of the Department of Juvenile Corrections.

On the night of August 21, 17 young offenders fled Sunnydale Farm in Nebraska while the minimum security facility burned to the ground in a blaze that is now considered caused by arson. Aiden Falconer, 15, is the prime suspect in that fire.

He and his sister, Margaret, 11, were placed in the Juvenile Corrections system for their own protection after their parents received life sentences for aiding and abetting foreign terrorists. The Falconer children were last seen in the resort town of Colchester in northern Vermont. . . .

The boy stepped timidly into the lobby of the Red Jacket Motor Lodge. He looked about fifteen or sixteen, tall and thin, with short dark hair.

"What can I do for you, son?" the desk clerk asked.

"This might sound weird." The boy's shorts and T-shirt were ragged and dirty, but so many kids dressed that way these days that the clerk barely noticed. "My uncle Frank stayed in this hotel. Nine years ago."

"You're sure? That's a long time."

The teen nodded earnestly. "It was my birthday. I was six. But he's kind of lost touch with the family, so my mom wanted me to ask if maybe you still have his address on the computer."

"We're not allowed to give out guest information," the man said. "Not even after nine years."

"Are you sure?" the boy wheedled. "It would really mean a lot to my mom. She hasn't seen her brother since forever."

"Sorry," the desk clerk told him. "Hotel rules."

As the disappointed boy slunk out of the lobby, the man wondered if perhaps he should alert the police about the young visitor with the strange request. After all, there had been fugitives spotted in the area — the children of those notorious Falconers. And wasn't the older one a teenager?

But this had been a lone kid, not a pair. Besides, people who are running from the cops don't walk into public places to make unusual requests. This was nothing — just a summer family trying to track down a long-lost relative.

Had the desk clerk been paying closer attention, he would have seen the teenager jog not to a waiting car but around the side of the building to the narrow ravine behind the motel. There, Aiden Falconer found his sister, Meg, crouched in the underbrush.

"It's a no-go," he reported sadly. "The guy's a stickler."

"It figures." Meg pulled from her pocket a weathered photo that showed a young man and woman sunning in lounge chairs on the pool deck of this very hotel.

The man had long red hair and a beard. Frank Lindenauer — Uncle Frank, they had once called him. He was much more than a family friend. He was their parents' CIA handler. Frank Lindenauer had convinced the husband-and-wife criminologist team of John and Louise Falconer to develop profiles to help American agents identify terrorist sleeper cells.

Meg shuddered at the thought. What had gone wrong? How had the Falconers' profiles fallen into the hands of the very terrorists they had been designed to defeat?

Maybe Lindenauer knew. He was the only person who could prove that the Falconers had been working for the CIA the whole time. They weren't traitors . . . they were *patriots*. If only they could have found him before the trial.

Stop! Meg commanded herself. That kind of thinking was useless. It made her sad. Worse, it made her weak — the one thing she and Aiden couldn't afford to be if they were going to get their parents out of prison and clear their names.

"Listen," Meg said determinedly. "The information we need is on that computer in there. It's our only lead. Without it we're dead in the water. If that desk clerk was a thousand-pound grizzly bear, we couldn't let him stop us!"

"I agree," Aiden said readily. "But what can we do? Knock him out with a tire iron?"

Meg was stubborn. "If that's what it takes."

"Be serious!"

Meg thought it over. "Stay hidden, but keep an eye on the office. When the guy leaves, that's our chance."

Aiden looked dubious. "But what if he doesn't leave?"

"He'll leave. Trust me."

Meg walked along the narrow dirt lane that separated the back of the motel from the woods. She kept an eye on the row of identical bathroom windows in the facade of cedar shakes.

Closed . . . closed . . . closed . . . jackpot.

The metal sash was raised a couple of inches. Meg peered inside. No toothbrushes or toiletries on the vanity. Beyond the bathroom door, two made beds.

Nobody home.

She pushed the window open and hoisted herself up and in.

Smoke detector right over the bed. Perfect.

She pulled a box of matches from her pocket, struck one, and held it to the corner of the yellow pages under the nightstand. There was instant combustion. She climbed onto the bed and held the blazing directory like a torch to the smoke alarm.

The siren went off almost immediately. Meg jumped down, rushed to the bathroom, and tossed the flaming phone book into the toilet bowl. Then she wriggled back out through the window and hit the ground running.

2

When the alarm went off, Aiden reacted with shock. A fire? Now?

Or — he watched the desk clerk rush out of the office — Meg's plan in action?

Typical Meg — using an M-1 tank to swat a mosquito. He hoped she wasn't crazy enough to burn down the motel.

He sprinted into the office, where the wailing Klaxon was cranked way beyond the tolerance level. Wincing, he ducked behind the desk and pounced on the computer.

GUEST FILES. He clicked the tab for nine years before. Under NAME SEARCH, he typed LINDENAUER.

SEARCH RESULTS = 0.

Aiden frowned. What was going on here?

Lindenauer wasn't the simplest name in the world. Maybe it had been entered wrong. He tried a few possible misspellings: *Lyndenauer . . . Lindennauer . . . Lindinauer . . .*

Nothing.

Meg appeared at his arm. "Find it?" She had to shout to be heard.

Aiden shook his head and kept trying. *Linde-nower . . . Lindenour . . .*

"What if he didn't pay?" Meg suggested.

"What?"

"He'd only be on the computer if he was the one who paid for the room," Meg reasoned. "Maybe his girlfriend paid. What was her name?"

"Aunt — " Another problem. Uncle Frank had a lot of girlfriends. All of them had been introduced as Aunt Somebody. Even Mom and Dad used to have trouble telling them apart. They had referred to Lindenauer's many relationships as the soap opera. The joke had turned agonizingly unfunny during the trial. In their attempts to find the CIA agent himself, the Falconers' lawyers had tracked down a handful of his exes — a gaggle of aunts. But no uncle.

Aiden frowned. He was missing something important. The last year and a half had been just a blur, but not the trial. He remembered everything about *that* — every word, every detail, right down to the jingling of their parents' leg irons as they were led away for the final time. How could anybody forget the end of the world?

When he'd been away from the courtroom, he'd pored over the transcripts, memorizing the testimony he'd missed. He especially recalled the desperate meetings with Mom, Dad, and the lawyers as they scrambled to come up with evidence, no matter how flimsy, that Frank Lindenauer existed and had worked for the CIA. The parade of exes — Aunt Brigitte, Aunt Caroline, Aunt Trudy . . .

He had a murky vision of a tall brunette holding out a wrapped present. His heart skipped a beat. *My birthday! My sixth birthday!*

Aiden's birthday was July 24th. They had celebrated in Vermont! The missing ex was the girlfriend in the picture! What was her name? Aunt —

Come on! Think!

"Jane! Aunt Jane!"

"Jane what?" Meg demanded.

"I don't know!" He typed in JANE.

SEARCH RESULTS = 39.

He narrowed the time frame to July.

SEARCH RESULTS = 4.

A quartet of records filled the screen. Only one fell over July 24th:

JANE MACINTOSH, 240 EAST UNIVERSITY STREET, #23C, BOSTON, MASSACHUSETTS.

"That's the one."

Meg scribbled the address down on a sheet of hotel stationery and stuffed it in her pocket. "We're golden!"

And then a fire engine squealed into the hotel parking lot, sirens blaring.

3

They fled, pounding for the trees as uniformed firefighters jumped down from the pumper.

The desk clerk came running from the opposite direction. "Stop those kids!"

But Aiden and Meg had already reached the cover of the ravine.

"Please tell me the hotel isn't on fire," panted Aiden, sidestepping trees left and right.

"I just set off the alarm," Meg gasped in reply. "It must call the fire department automatically."

They burst out the other side of the woods and made for their getaway vehicle — a stolen four-wheeler parked in the low brush at the edge of a farmer's field.

They jumped on, and Aiden gunned the engine. The quad roared to life and sprang forward, bouncing on the uneven ground. In no time, they were up to fifty miles an hour, and the combination of wind and rough ride threatened to fling them off the seat.

"Hang on!" cried Aiden.

In thirty seconds, they were across the property, crashing through a weathered corral fence into an apple orchard. A phalanx of sturdy trunks seemed to leap out at them. Aiden wheeled to the right, nearly flipping the quad over. At the last instant, he recovered and blasted down a narrow alley between the trees.

They flew through the orchard, the all-terrain vehicle's speedometer inching toward sixty. The road loomed dead ahead. Suddenly, four squad cars whizzed past, lights flashing.

Aiden killed the motor, and they lurched to a halt. There they sat, barely breathing, as the wailing sirens faded into the distance.

"Think they'll come back?" Meg whispered in his ear.

"I doubt they saw us." But he was ready to flee at the faintest hint of the cruisers returning.

A very long sixty seconds passed. At last, Aiden gunned the engine, and they were off again, jouncing over the tarmac and into the open country on the other side.

While the authorities prowled the grid of roads and highways, the quad carried the Falconers across farms and fields, far from the patrols and roadblocks designed to capture them. The vehicle was so ideal for their getaway that Aiden almost forgave himself for boosting it in the first place.

Fugitive 101 — don't feel guilty about breaking the law. It's the only way to survive.

Yet the stealing, lying, and running from police left a bad taste in his mouth. Meg wasn't as squeamish. She could shrug it off as necessary. She even saw a vague future time when they would make it all right again. Was she ignorant, or just young? Aiden couldn't be sure, but he knew he didn't share her simple optimism.

They headed east — at least they guessed it was east. As they rode, the terrain became rockier. There were no more farms, just small hillside orchards. They crossed roads cluttered with billboards advertising ski resorts. Everywhere they looked, mountains lay ahead.

Aiden aimed the quad at the valleys between peaks. But even there, the terrain rose steeply. The huge tires jerked and trembled as the vehicle negotiated the boulder-strewn ground. Meg clung to Aiden, and Aiden clung to the handlebars. The world tilted upward. The speedometer needle trembled barely above zero.

This isn't driving. It's motorized rock climbing!

They forged onward, ascending a narrow ridge that rose above a picturesque landscape. Higher up, Aiden could make out a ski lodge. Below was a small neighborhood of condos. It was a spectacular spot, but Aiden was nervous.

"If we have to go back, there's no way we'll have the space to turn this thing around!" he called over his shoulder.

Meg shared none of his trepidation. "Why would we have to go back?"

"What if the ridge ends in a hundred-foot cliff?"

"You think too much, bro!" Meg exclaimed. "We're doing fine. This is the only way to travel."

With that, the ATV's big motor sputtered, coughed, and went silent. Aiden twisted the key in the starter. The engine caught for a second and then died again. The quad, no longer under its own power, keeled over sideways. The seat tilted up and around, until the two riders were hanging on for dear life.

"What happened?" cried Meg. "What's going on?"

Heart sinking, Aiden caught a glimpse of the fuel gauge. "We're out of gas!"

"How could you not notice something like that?"

she yelled in Aiden's ear as gravity and the angle of the quad pressed her into his back.

"What was I supposed to do? Pull into a gas station?"

"Yeah, but — *uh-oh*!"

They both felt the tipping point a split second before the quad toppled over.

"Jump!" Aiden cried.

They threw themselves free just as the vehicle rolled. Aiden found a handhold on an outcropping of rock, but Meg began to slide. He watched in terror as the half ton of metal first skidded and then bounced down the slope, coming up on Meg from behind.

"Duck!"

It struck a boulder and was propelled up. Meg stared in horror. For an instant, the ATV blotted out the sun as it sailed over her, spraying her with stray bolts and fiberglass fragments. She tucked in her head, arms, and legs — and prayed.

Crash!

4

Aiden let go of the handhold, digging in his heels in an attempt to control his descent. The plan succeeded too well. He jolted to a sudden stop and somersaulted over. All at once, he was rolling. The world around him became a twirling blur of stone and sky, but he did manage to catch sight of his tumbling sister twenty feet ahead of him.

"Meg!" He could not tell if the careening ATV had hit her — only that it was past her now, bashing itself to pieces as it caromed down. He barely noticed his own jolts and scrapes as the uneven rock surface brutalized him. His sister was all that mattered.

Then he was in the brush, brambles and twigs grazing his skin. The vegetation slowed him to the point where he could clamp his hands around the trunk of a juniper bush. He hauled himself to his feet, scanning the scrub for Meg.

She lay at the bottom of a small hollow, just a few feet away from the wreckage of the ATV. She wasn't moving.

Careful not to lose balance again, he sidestepped down the grade to her. His dread easily overpowered any pain he might be feeling from his trip down the mountain. This predicament — their parents in jail; he and Meg running for their lives — the one thing that made it even remotely bearable was the fact that Aiden and Meg were in it together.

There was a faint groan, and Meg turned her scratched and dirty face up to regard him. "I'm always waiting around for you," she complained. "You're slowing me down, bro."

"Are you okay?"

"Barely." She struggled unsteadily to her feet. "That tin-plated piece of junk missed me by, like, three inches. I could be a smudge on that rock up there."

"Can you walk?" Aiden asked in concern. "Because I don't think there's another way out of here."

His sister took two experimental steps. "Maybe we should head for those ski condos. We're both in need of repairs."

Aiden looked ruefully at the remains of the ATV.

"Talk about repairs! We've had to steal stuff before, but this is the first time we've totaled anything. Somebody's out one quad."

"We can't think about that," Meg reminded him quickly.

He was not consoled. "Well, what am I supposed to think about?"

"Think about helping Mom and Dad," she suggested. "Think about Jane Macintosh. Think about getting to Boston."

They trudged across rocky ground in the direction of the neighborhood they had seen from the ridge. It felt good to be moving again, despite the aches and stings of their injuries.

They made their way in silence for a while, and then Meg asked, "Where do you think we are?"

It was a good question. Back in Colchester, the whole world was looking for them. The police had put out an APB. The search was probably doubled now, after the near miss at the Red Jacket Motor Lodge. Had they put enough distance between themselves and that heavy heat? Could they talk to people and ask directions without worrying they might be recognized?

"We probably made it fifty miles or more," he estimated. "But Vermont's pretty small. We should avoid the locals if we can. At least until we get out of the state."

They crested a small rise and gazed over the neighborhood of ski chalets. An ancient rusted pickup truck that was once blue rattled onto the road below. The spry old fellow who jumped out was at least sixty years older than the truck, and plainly agitated.

"I can't believe you two are walking! I've never seen such a fall in all my born days! Are you all right?"

"Oh, it looked worse than it was," Meg said cheerfully, hoping there wasn't too much visible blood running from her many cuts.

"We're totally fine," Aiden added. "Thanks anyway."

The man shook his head in disgust. "What were your parents thinking, letting you ride off on that newfangled buzz bomb?"

The Falconers exchanged a look. What was probably going through their parents' minds at this moment was a combination of *How did this happen to us?* and *How are we going to survive it?* What else was there to think about in prison?

"Don't worry about us," Meg said airily. "We can walk home from here."

"Walk, nothing," the old man said stubbornly. "I'm taking you to the hospital."

"But we're okay," Aiden protested, alarmed. "Just a few bumps — "

"Then the doctor can send you home. Get in the truck." He opened the driver's door and climbed inside.

They hesitated. "Should we run?" whispered Meg.

Aiden shook his head imperceptibly. "Then he might call the cops."

"But what if someone at the hospital recognizes us?"

"Take it easy. We walk inside, he drives away, we walk back out again."

They piled in and the truck backfired to life. Their chauffeur proceeded down the road at eight miles an hour, staring through his cracked windshield with dogged concentration.

The silence was so uncomfortable that Aiden felt he had to say something. "I hope we're not taking you out of your way."

It opened up the floodgates. "I had to go into

town anyway. The Andersons need a new ball cock for their toilet. I'm the handyman hereabouts. The only one, as a matter of fact — Lester Mercure's the name. That's like Mercury, but with an 'e' instead of a 'y' — French, you know. . . ."

By the time they'd pulled up in front of the small medical center in the town of St. Johnsbury, the Falconers knew much of Lester Mercure's life story, plus much of the private business of the "city slickers" who owned the ski condos in the area.

Aiden opened the passenger door. "Well, thanks for the ride. Uh — we owe you one."

The handyman got out of the truck himself and began shepherding them toward Emergency. "I'm coming in there with you."

"But what about the Andersons' toilet?" blurted Meg.

"I saw what happened," the old man said stubbornly. "The doctor might need to talk to me."

Aiden and Meg had no choice but to allow themselves to be escorted inside to the check-in desk. Aiden gave his name as Gary Donovan — one of his fellow inmates at Sunnydale Farm, the juvenile detention facility he and his sister had escaped from. Meg used another Sunnydale identity, Belinda Gustafson, the toughest, meanest girl in the dormitory. It made sense to pretend they were unrelated. The police would be looking for a brother and sister.

And then Lester put his two cents in. "I saw the whole thing," he told the admitting nurse. "They were riding on this mechanized whatchamacallit, when it tipped over and threw them off the ridge. Darned near scared me to death. I thought I'd be cleaning up the bodies."

They took seats in the waiting room among a few other patients. To their dismay, Lester came with them. Meg cast Aiden an agonized look. How would they ever get out of this place under the watchful eye of this well-meaning old bore?

They waited until Aiden thought he would go insane. Somewhere in this town, buses were departing for Boston, home of Jane Macintosh, who might know where to find Frank Lindenauer. A bus might be leaving at that very moment. . . .

And what are we doing?

Sitting in a hospital with Lester Mercure, with an "e," not a "y."

A police officer came into Emergency, and Aiden nearly jumped out of his skin.

Calm down. He's just filing a report on some car accident. He isn't looking for fugitives.

At long last, a nurse called for Donovan and

Gustafson. Lester accompanied them to the open door.

"Are you family?" the nurse asked him.

"No, but I witnessed the incident firsthand. Darnedest thing I ever saw. They were riding up a mountain on some kind of cockamamie dune buggy — "

"Why don't you wait in the lounge where you'll be comfortable?" she suggested, her tone polite but firm.

Aiden and Meg were pathetically grateful. The nurse escorted them to two separate exam rooms and told them the doctor would be right in.

Aiden waited a few seconds for her to walk away before running next door. Meg had the same idea, and the two collided in the hall.

"Let's blow this Popsicle stand," urged Meg.

"Right."

They couldn't leave through the waiting room — Lester would be sitting right there. They walked briskly down the brightly lit corridor, slaloming around medical center employees and rolling equipment carts. Luckily, the place was busy, and the doctors and nurses who rushed to and fro had little time to think about a couple of kids.

All at once, Meg let out a little gasp and stopped

short. Aiden followed the twitch of her gesturing elbow. In the center of a bulletin board plastered with hospital announcements was tacked a blotchy fax with two small photographs.

Aiden recognized the murky images immediately.

Our mug shots from Sunnydale!

5

They were being hunted — even here, on the opposite end of the state.

They had to get out of Vermont. But that was putting the cart before the horse. First they had to get out of the hospital.

They increased their pace, turning left and left again, following the path of the corridor. Although the medical center wasn't huge, the endless halls were like a maze, with no windows to the outside. Heavy glass doors led to different wards and departments. Aiden's eyes darted from sign to sign: RADIOLOGY, MATERNITY, INTENSIVE CARE, AUTHORIZED PERSONNEL ONLY — where was EXIT?

"How do you get out of this dump?" Meg hissed.

Aiden shrugged helplessly. Was that Emergency coming up again?

Oh, no! We've been walking in circles!

All at once, their nurse stepped out of one of the

empty exam rooms, looking around in concern for her young patients.

Not knowing what else to do, Aiden grabbed Meg by the arm and yanked her through a pair of steel security doors. They felt the heat of the afternoon — they were outside the building. But this was no exit. They were in a narrow loading bay. Two white-coated med techs were climbing into the front of a waiting ambulance, its motor running.

One of them activated the siren. It resounded like a bomb blast in the confines of the loading bay. The earsplitting sound seemed to jump-start Meg. She ran up, unlatched the rear doors, and leaped aboard.

Aiden tried to follow her just as the ambulance lurched forward. His hand closed on the metal handle, and he found himself hanging off the back of the accelerating vehicle, floundering on the open door.

"Meg, help me!"

She waited for him to swing around and grabbed two fistfuls of his T-shirt. "Let go!" she ordered, and wrestled him inside. They collapsed in a heap on the metal floor.

The hospital's access road whipped by as they picked up speed.

From a kneeling position, Aiden managed to reach out and pull the door shut. "I hope you have a plan."

The ambulance swerved around a corner, flinging the two of them against a rack of oxygen tanks. Meg steadied herself against a wall-mounted stretcher. "We're *out*, bro!"

"We're in a moving ambulance!" Aiden exclaimed.

She shrugged. "It has to stop eventually."

"Yeah, but what if that happens forty miles out in the woods? Then how do we get to a bus station?" Aiden peered out the rear window. The short downtown strip of St. Johnsbury flashed by in the scratched glass.

All at once, the wail of the siren was replaced by a series of staccato blurps as the ambulance slowed in a cluster of traffic.

Aiden made a split-second decision. "Jump."

He yanked on the hatch and was just about to push it open when he saw the police car. It turned in from the intersection and fell into line right behind them.

The effort to keep the doors from flying wide open nearly tore his shoulder in two. The cruiser pulled even with them and then passed on the left.

Aiden knew this might be their last chance. "Now!" He unlatched the doors, and he and Meg bailed out. With another blurp of the siren, the ambulance sprung away, its open hatch rattling. The Falconers hopped up on the sidewalk and looked around furtively. No one was pointing and yelling at them. Their escape had gone unnoticed.

"Bus station," murmured Aiden.

"Right."

The walk was nerve-racking. Every glance from a passerby set Aiden's mind racing. Was that recognition? And what kind of recognition? *Did you hear about the two kids who jumped out of an ambulance? Did you hear about the two kids who ran away from the hospital?*

Worst of all, what if somebody connected the two kids from those stories with the two kids who were wanted by police on the other side of the state?

His imagination conjured up a crowded bus terminal filled with patrolling policemen, prying eyes, and suspicious questions. But the "station" turned out to be a Plexiglas shelter on the far end of town. A disintegrating hand-scrawled cardboard sign declared BUY TICKETS AT OWEN'S.

Owen's was the luncheonette across the street. A counterman who concealed a sumo-size potbelly under a greasy white apron presided over ticket sales and "the best chowder in New England."

Throughout the transaction, Aiden expected the man to burst out with, *Why are you two going to Boston on your own? Where are your parents? What's the deal here?*

But all he asked them was, "You guys want some french fries to go?"

The bad news was, the next bus to Boston was the Moonlight Special. It didn't leave until midnight.

They split a take-out hamburger and a cup of chowder in the woods behind the bus stop. "One thing about life on the run," Aiden mumbled as he wolfed down his half. "There's never time to eat."

"Tell me about it," Meg agreed, polishing off the soup. "We should start the Fugitive Diet. You know, sic the FBI on fat people and see how much weight they lose. We'll get rich."

"Yeah, well, we sure aren't rich now," Aiden said glumly. "In Boston, we're going to have to figure out a way to get our hands on some cash."

"Maybe Jane What's-her-face will lend us some," Meg suggested hopefully. "She's our 'aunt,' after all."

Aiden grimaced. "I'll be happy if she knows what happened to Frank Lindenauer."

"Amen to that."

They remained under cover of the woods until nightfall and then moved to a small park beside the bus stop. Just past midnight, they boarded an air-conditioned Greyhound to Boston. Meg sank into a padded seat near the back and closed her eyes.

"No sleeping," Aiden ordered.

"Aw, come on," she protested. "It's the Moonlight Special. You're supposed to sleep."

"If the cops stop the bus, we have to be ready to run for it."

"The cops think we're still in Colchester. Nobody knows we're here."

He was adamant. "No sleeping."

By the time the bus had left the town limits, both Falconers were dead to the world.

6

Agent Emmanuel Harris of the FBI took a sip from the steaming cup and nearly gagged. Ugh! What passed for coffee in these small-town police stations tasted more like raw sewage. Hadn't these people ever heard of Starbucks?

Chief Bumgartner of the Colchester PD hooked his thumbs in his pants pockets. "What do you say, Harris? Time to take down the roadblocks?"

Harris barely had the strength to shake his head. It was nearly three in the morning. Except for a ninety-minute catnap on a too-short cot in one of the holding cells, he'd been going nonstop for forty-eight hours. "It's too soon."

"Can't be too soon for me," the chief informed him. "A department our size hasn't got the man-power for this kind of operation. Unless," he added, "you bureau hotshots want to send us some extra bodies to work the checkpoints."

Harris did his best to fold his six-foot-seven frame

into a chair designed for someone half his size. "I wish I could. This case isn't under FBI jurisdiction. It belongs to Juvenile Corrections."

"So what's the big deal about a couple of kids? Even if their names happen to be Falconer" — Bumgartner's face turned suddenly urgent — "you don't think they're working for their folks, do you? Finishing what their parents started?"

"No, nothing like that," Harris said with a sigh.

How could he ever explain it? That Emmanuel Harris, the hero who had brought to justice the most notorious traitors of the past half century, lay awake nights wondering if the right people were in prison.

The FBI was certain that John and Louise Falconer were guilty. Harris wished he shared their confidence. And that wasn't the only thing weighing on his mind.

If John and Louise Falconer turned out to be innocent, that meant their son and daughter were on the run, risking their lives, thanks to the Bureau's mistake.

Thanks to Harris's mistake.

"How about twelve more hours?" he bargained. "We've got them. I can feel it. How could they get past those roadblocks?"

One of the younger officers hung up the phone. "Chief, that was Tom Vickers out on Route 3. Says his quad bike is missing."

The next thing Aiden knew, a hand was shaking him out of a deep sleep.

"Kid, wake up."

With effort, he raised a single heavy eyelid. The driver of the Moonlight Special stood over him. "Boston. Last stop."

"Five more minutes," pleaded a slumbering Meg beside him.

Aiden squinted out the window at the dimly lit terminal. "What time is it?"

"Quarter to five," the driver informed him. He seemed pleased. "We're twenty minutes early." He examined them closely. "That's why there's nobody here to meet you, right?"

"Great." Meg opened a wary eye. "We're early, and Dad's always late."

Aiden was filled with admiration. Even half asleep, his little sister was right on the ball. "Come on, Belinda," he told her. "Let's get some breakfast."

They scrambled off the Greyhound and were gone before the driver could comment on their lack of luggage.

Keeping their faces down, they hurried out of the terminal. A bus station was the last place fugitives should be hanging around. But that left them in a near-deserted inner city in the middle of the night. It was more than a little creepy — concrete jungle, dark streets, shady characters . . .

Oh, grow up! Meg scolded herself. *After everything that's happened, getting mugged is the least of our worries!*

She pulled the crumpled paper out of her pocket. "Two-forty East University Street, apartment twenty-three C. I hope Aunt Jane likes an early wake-up call."

Aiden frowned. "Where can we find a city map at this hour?"

"I've got a better idea." With grim determination, Meg strode out into the middle of the road, threw up her arm, and yelled, *"Taxi!"*

Almost immediately, a Shamrock cab appeared out of nowhere and pulled up beside her.

"Where to, kid?"

"Two-forty East University," Meg replied. She beckoned to Aiden. "You coming?"

Reluctantly, he got in beside her. "We've only got eighteen dollars!" he hissed. "What if it isn't enough?"

She shrugged. "We stole an ATV and drove it off a mountain. Why are you stressing over stiffing a cabdriver a couple of bucks?"

The ride only cost them twelve. But their relief quickly turned to dismay; 240 East University Street was an enclosed mini-mall in the middle of a long block of seedy storefronts.

"She lives *here*?" Meg exclaimed as the cab pulled away.

The flyspecked glass door was unlocked, but the stores and offices inside were empty and dark. Unit 23C was on the basement level opposite the only establishment that was open for business — a twenty-four-hour pawnshop.

Arrow Travel was a tiny agency with a single desk surrounded by posters of Greek islands and Alaskan glaciers. Racks of brochures stood against the back wall.

Meg was as quick to despair as she was to action. "I must have written the address down wrong! I could strangle myself! That was our only clue!"

"No, look." Aiden pointed through the window. On the neat desk sat a brass nameplate: JANE MACINTOSH. "She gave the hotel her work address. She's a travel agent. This is the right place!"

Meg had already moved on to the next disaster.

Hung around the inside doorknob was a sign: CLOSED UNTIL MONDAY.

Aiden followed her gaze. "Oh, come *on*!" he exclaimed in consternation. "Friday hasn't even started yet. How could they be closed up for the weekend?"

"It looks like she's running a one-woman show in there," Meg concluded. "I guess if she's the boss and all the employees, she sets the schedule, too."

There was an old-fashioned phone booth outside the pawnshop. The directory was dog-eared but still intact. Jane Macintosh was not listed.

"Why can't anything ever be easy?" Aiden lamented. "This should be her house, and she's happy to see us, and Frank Lindenauer is her next-door neighbor!"

"What are you getting so worked up about?" Meg soothed. "We found her. All we have to do is hang out till Monday and she'll be here."

"We have six bucks in the world, Meg, and no place to sleep. How can we live for three days on six bucks?"

"We had zero when we ran away from Sunnydale," his sister reminded him.

"That was in the middle of a Nebraska cornfield. This is a crowded city. We can't live on the street here. It's too dangerous!"

"You're right about that," she admitted. "If we're going to make it to Monday, we'll need some money. Okay, how do we get it?"

"Not by stealing," Aiden said quickly.

"That leaves work," his sister decided. "We'll do odd jobs."

"*I'll* do odd jobs," Aiden corrected. "I can pass for older. A kid your age trying to earn money would look suspicious."

Meg was incensed. "What am I supposed to do — twiddle my thumbs when I could be helping out?"

"You've got the most important job of all," Aiden argued. "It's up to you to find a hotel we can afford."

By this time it was daylight, and the streets were beginning to fill with early-bird commuters. Aiden and Meg split a bagel and juice and sat in a small outdoor café, watching Boston come alive around them.

Just after seven, a dusty landscaping truck, towing an equipment trailer, stopped at the curb. A group of four young men in work clothes hopped aboard the flatbed and tapped on the roof of the cab to signal that they were ready to go.

The driver stuck his head out. "Where's Rankin?"

"Sick," replied one of the crew.

The foreman was disgusted. "He gets conveniently sick on Fridays. We've got eleven houses to do in Brookline, and we're shorthanded."

The worker shrugged. "He said he'd try to send a replacement."

"Oh, yeah, you can really depend on Rankin. How long are we supposed to wait for this replacement? All day?"

Aiden jumped up. "Meet me here at five," he whispered to Meg. Then he was over the wrought-iron railing, across the sidewalk, and onto the trailer.

"Sorry I'm late. Rankin sent me."

The boss regarded him dubiously. "Where'd he find you — the day care center?"

"I start Harvard in the fall," Aiden lied defensively.

"Okay, college boy. The pay's twelve bucks an hour, cash. No dental plan. Got it?"

"Fine." It sounded better than fine. It sounded like survival — at least for one more day.

7

Meg remained at the café for a long time. In a style that reminded her of her cautious, practical brother, she took microscopic bites of her half of the bagel, making it last. She wasn't easily intimidated, but the thought of finding a hotel in this huge city was something she would have given much to avoid. What could they afford, after all? Some crumbling fleabag full of roaches and rats? And who knew what kind of sleazy business went on in places like that? There could be bullets flying through the paper-thin walls.

She built this line of thinking into a pretty sizable grudge against Aiden for deserting her here. But to be fair, it really wouldn't have worked any other way. How was an eleven-year-old supposed to make money — by robbing a bank? On the other hand, would scouting out hotel rooms appear any less weird for a young girl? How many sixth-graders hung around seedy neighborhoods, strolling from flophouse to flophouse, comparison shopping?

There had to be a better way. If she was home and had her laptop, she could just go online and price every hotel in Boston in a matter of minutes. She grimaced. Her laptop, along with everything else she owned, was in the storage facility of the Department of Juvenile Corrections in Washington, DC. She'd probably never see it again.

Suddenly, she had the answer. Her laptop may have been gone forever, but the Internet was still open for business. All she had to do was find a way to get on the Web.

It was so simple — the library! They offered free Internet access to the public.

I'm the public!

Didn't it figure — the cashier had no idea where the nearest library was. But a customer pointed her in the direction of the Cliffhaven branch, just a few blocks away, opening at nine.

The two-hundred-year-old building was spectacular, almost a miniature castle, built around a high stone turret. Inside, however, it could have been any library in the world — rows of beige metal shelving, faded carpeting, and well-worn oak tables and chairs.

The computers were behind the periodical section. Since it was early, she had no problem snagging a cubicle.

She searched keywords BOSTON and LODGING, and soon navigated her way onto a hotel site. She selected her price range — the lowest — and began to scroll through the possibilities.

They looked "scuzzy." That was her mother's word to describe hotels where the musty smell told the whole story. For Mom, mustiness implied a vast list of other failings — dirt, mildew, germs, infestation — all of them deal breakers.

I wonder if it's musty in jail. . . .

No. That line of thinking had to be cut off right away, before she ended up in tears.

She concentrated on the task at hand. The real problem was that even the inexpensive hotels were pretty expensive. After all, ninety bucks per night may have been a great bargain for Boston, but not if you didn't have the ninety bucks.

She sighed glumly. There were probably plenty of places cheaper than that, but they weren't the kind of establishments that advertised on the Web. Those hotels could be accessed only by walking down a garbage-strewn street to a front door reinforced with wire grating.

It was her first time online since the foster homes they'd lived in before Sunnydale. As if propelled by an irresistible force, her fingers began to meander around the keyboard, doing what she had promised herself she would never do. Back on the Google home page, she typed in the most infamous last name in America — Falconer.

The response was overwhelming: one-point-five-million hits. Each link held some special kind of torture. Pictures of the trial, that nightmare circus — the vengeful faces of the jurors; the angry bias in the judge's eyes; the steely indifference of that towering FBI agent — Harris, the man who had ruined all their lives; Mom and Dad in prison jumpsuits . . .

Oh, Mom, you always hated orange!

But the news updates weren't the worst of it. The letters — the postings on personal Web pages and blogs — were so vicious, they sent chills down her spine. "Hang 'em high," "bring back the electric chair," "burn that scum alive," "killing's too good for them."

Why are you reading this? she demanded of herself. *These morons don't know our family. They have no idea what they're talking about!*

Yet, like a rubbernecker at an accident scene, she

could not look away. She tried to convince herself that these opinions belonged to a few crackpots. But deep down she knew that the postings genuinely represented how people in the country felt about the Falconers.

Everybody believes they worked for terrorists! I'd hate them myself if I didn't know the truth!

If you need any more evidence that our justice system is broken, consider the fact that John and Louise Falconer were not executed and are living at taxpayers' expense in prison. Now it seems pretty obvious that their children, their teenage son at least, were their accomplices. Why else would two minors escape from their youth farm by burning the place to the ground, without giving so much as a thought to the many lives they put in danger?

Meg pulled up short. *That's us!*

Of course, she and Aiden knew that their escape had been reported in the news. But they'd always assumed it was a local story — in Nebraska, where Sunnydale was; in Chicago, where they'd been chased by police; and in Vermont, where a terrifying stranger they'd nicknamed Hairless Joe had suddenly appeared and tried to kill them.

This was different. Now they were becoming part of their parents' story, the desperado children of public enemies one and two.

That couldn't be good. The key to surviving as a fugitive was staying invisible. Being kids made it hard enough — they were constantly explaining why they were on their own. But if this somehow turned into *Falconers: The Sequel*, they were going to be more famous than Bonnie and Clyde. They wouldn't be able to walk down the street without half a dozen people dialing nine one one on their cell phones. There'd be zero chance of saving Mom and Dad then.

There's a solution to all this, she reminded herself, scrolling farther down. *Keep off the Internet. You'll only drive yourself crazy.*

Anyway, not all the one-point-five-million hits were about Mom and Dad. There were also some Web sites about falconry and falconry schools. There was a Falconer Center for the Performing Arts in Liverpool, England, and a luxury yacht called *The Falconer* that was available for rental . . . fascinating stuff. Yeah, right.

Her eyes wandered from the links to the ads that dotted the screen: fad diets, dating services, *Join Trans-Atlantica SkyPoints, America's #1 Frequent Flyer Program* . . .

She was amazed at the surge of warmth that took hold in her gut. Her parents used to travel extensively on the lecture circuit. Both of them had zillions of miles piled up with various airlines, including Trans-Atlantica. It was almost as if she had come upon a piece of her parents on the Web.

A thought occurred to her. After the trial, the government had padlocked the Falconers' home and frozen their assets and bank accounts. But what about frequent-flyer programs? Had the FBI shut those down as well?

She clicked on the link to the Trans-Atlantica site and typed in her father's name. A PIN was required, but that was easy. The password used by all the Falconers for everything was Mugsy, a tribute to an old family pet.

When the account information appeared on the screen, Meg had to hold herself back from cheering. *In your face, Agent Harris. You didn't think of everything!*

The idea struck her so abruptly that she was almost swept off her chair: *I wonder if there's a way to use these miles to book us a hotel room in Boston.*

The disappointment was instant. That would be really smart — checking in with a reservation booked in the name of a front-page traitor. That would be perfect for two kids trying not to be noticed.

Then it hit her. Mom! She had as many points as Dad. But she had always traveled under her maiden name, Louise Graham.

Excitedly, Meg called up her mother's frequent-flyer account using the same PIN. She whistled admiringly. Mom had more than seven hundred thousand SkyPoints.

That'll do, she thought to herself with a smile that was rare these days. *That'll do very nicely.*

Aiden slunk through the crowded downtown sidewalks, the soles of his sneakers barely lifting off the concrete. He had never been so exhausted in his life. Even the escape from Sunnydale — countless hours of fleeing through cornfields — hadn't left him in this much pain. The raking/pruning/lifting/hauling/pushing/bending of the landscaping work had strained muscles he hadn't even known existed. The simple act of sidestepping a hot dog vendor's cart required so much concentration that he thought he might pass out from the effort.

He hoped Meg had been able to arrange for a place to spend the night. If he didn't find a bed to flop on soon, he was going to drop dead at any minute.

When he spotted her, perched on the wrought-iron railing of the café, the flood of relief that washed over him was astonishing. He'd been so wrapped up in his own misery, he'd given barely a thought to his little sister. There was nobody braver, stronger, and more capable, but she was still only eleven years old. Abandoning her in the middle of Boston with no food, no shelter, and a few lonely dollars would never have been his first choice. Seeing her there, safe and sound — *and a little too relaxed, if you ask me* — brought home just how worried he'd been about her.

"Sorry I'm late," he greeted breathlessly. "They dropped us off in a different place, and I couldn't find the café."

She was fresh as a daisy, sipping on a Coke. "No offense, bro, but you look like they dragged you behind the truck."

He was too weary to take offense. "Tell me we live somewhere."

She smiled knowingly. "Follow me."

Mercifully, it was only a ten-minute walk before they came to the elegant marquee of the Royal Bostonian Hotel. Aiden stared round-eyed as his sister marched in an elegant brassbound door held open by a liveried doorman.

"You're kidding," he whispered, awed by the gigantic crystal chandeliers in the opulent lobby.

"I got us a suite," she announced smugly.

He pulled her behind a marble pillar. "Are you *crazy*? We can't afford to breathe the air in this place, let alone stay here! You know what I earned today? Ninety-six bucks! That wouldn't buy you a closet in this palace!"

"Relax," she soothed. "It's taken care of."

"By whom?"

"By Mom."

He gawked at her. What was the matter with Meg? Had the strain of their family tragedy pushed her over the edge? Was she starting to lose it?

She took his hand and pulled him into the paneled elevator. When the door closed and they were alone, she explained how she had used Louise Graham's SkyPoints to book them a long weekend in a five-star hotel.

"I'm Belinda Graham, and you're my brother, Gary," she explained as the elevator opened onto the fourth-floor hall. "Louise is our mother, but she's in meetings all day. Check it out."

If Aiden had been surprised before, now he was thunderstruck. The Provincetown Suite looked like something out of a movie — a vast, elegantly appointed Victorian parlor and two luxurious bedrooms, featuring king-size canopy beds.

Aiden was overawed. "How many points did she have?"

"They upgraded me," Meg confided. "I'm adorable. The king of Spain stayed here last year — probably not on frequent-flyer miles."

Aiden regarded her with respect. "I can't believe you pulled this off. But you have to know it's risky. This suite can be traced to Mom."

She shrugged. "If the FBI didn't close down the frequent-flyer accounts during the trial, why would they remember them now?"

It made sense. Still — "But we're supposed to be keeping a low profile, Meg. You've got to know this isn't it."

She looked him straight in the eye. "Are our lives

so fantastic that we don't deserve to catch a break once in a blue moon? We're stuck until Monday. What does it hurt if we live a little?"

He looked behind her to the Jacuzzi tub in the gleaming marble bathroom. The soothing jets were on his aching muscles inside of five minutes.

Sleep.

There was no describing the depth and perfection of it. For days, the Falconers had been snatching catnaps in haylofts, boxcars, and buses. The nighttime was far too valuable to waste on rest. When all was dark and prying eyes were shut, that was the time to run, to flee.

But this, thought Meg through delicious dreams, *nowhere to go, nothing to accomplish but sleep, sleep, sleep, on a feathery bed in the best hotel in Boston —*

When the phone rang, she lifted several inches off the mattress and snatched up the receiver in hazy outrage. Still half asleep, she struggled to put together a stream of curses to howl at this inconsiderate —

A recorded voice came on the line: "This is your automated wake-up call. The time is now seven A.M."

Wake-up call?

That was when she saw Aiden bustling around

the palatial living room, pulling on his grass-stained T-shirt.

"What are you doing, bro? It's the middle of the night."

"I'm going to meet the crew," he told her.

"On Saturday?"

"They work seven days a week in the summer," he explained. "Tomorrow, too."

"But" — she could barely think straight — "but the room's already paid for. Why break your neck?"

"We still have to eat," Aiden reminded her. "Money means survival. Survival means a chance to help Mom and Dad." He paused at the door. "How do I look?"

"Disgusting," she replied honestly. "And you look better than you smell. Don't you think the crew's going to notice that your clothes reek?"

He shrugged. "Five minutes in the hot sun, and we'll all smell the same. But you've got a point." His shirt was ripped and filthy. When Meg took stock of her own clothing, she noted that her shorts were starting to unravel at the cuffs.

He produced four twenty-dollar bills and handed them to his sister. "Buy us some clothes. Nothing expensive, but if we look too gross, we'll attract attention."

"We'll attract *flies*," Meg amended sourly. She wrinkled her nose. "You already do. Get out of here, Aiden. Go make us rich."

The newspapers seemed to call out to Meg. She had been staring at them for twenty minutes now — ever since the bundle had been heaved from the back of a truck to the sidewalk beside the shuttered newsstand.

I can sell these. She recalled Aiden's words: *Money means survival.*

But as she stooped to grab the twine binding, an unpleasant voice declared, "You want a paper, you pay a buck like everybody else."

The newsstand owner was glaring at her as he undid the padlock on his curbside booth.

"Just reading the stock market report," she mumbled, and hurried away. That would be swell — to get arrested for swiping newspapers after coming so far. Aiden would kill her, and he'd be right to.

She stepped back through the polished brass entryway into the muted light of the elegant lobby. But was she any safer in here? Rich people had eyes, too, and so did snooty desk clerks and bellhops. After all, how many eleven-year-olds hung out in five-star hotels?

The thought had barely crossed her mind when the door to the coffee shop opened and out stepped a girl who looked exactly Meg's age and size. She was accompanied by her father; at least he appeared to be her father — a youngish man in a well-tailored pin-striped suit. The daughter was beautifully dressed as well, in pink denim pants and matching jacket. It was obvious these people belonged at the Royal Bostonian. They looked like an ad for a swank country club — clear-eyed, handsome, and wealthy. It made Meg even more conscious of her tattered shorts and T-shirt. Aiden was right — she and her brother needed something decent to wear, especially in a place like this.

There was only one flaw in the father-and-daughter portrait. The man looked busy and slightly impatient. And the girl was the picture of misery.

"I'll be in meetings all day, Chelsea," Meg heard him say, "so you're on your own until dinner. Don't waste the whole day in front of the TV."

Chelsea said something in an inaudible voice, never raising her eyes from the marble floor.

Her father frowned. "I have to go now. Use your time *well*."

He went outside and allowed the doorman to hail

him a taxi. The girl started for the elevators, head down, feet dragging.

Meg was surprised to feel a flush of anger toward this girl she had never even met. Where did Chelsea get off acting like the world had just ended? She should have been the happiest kid alive.

It was not the girl's fine clothes and money that brought out Meg's envy. It was this: Whatever the reason for her long face and sad eyes, Chelsea had something Meg could only dream about — the chance to be with her father.

Meg had never shopped at a secondhand store in her life. But the Back Bay Thrift Shop was just what she needed. New clothes seemed unnatural somehow — road-map creases along geometric folds.

Clothes should look lived in, not straight from the package.

The answer — buy lived-in clothes.

An added bonus: The thrift shop was really cheap. For Aiden's eighty dollars she was able to pick up shorts and jeans for both of them, an assortment of T-shirts and sweatshirts, and a pile of socks and underwear.

She was so pleased with herself that she waited for Aiden in the lobby so she could surprise him with the purchases as soon as he returned from work. *That's just what he needs*, she thought with a chuckle, *to be stalked with a bag full of boxers.*

The elevator doors parted, and out stepped Chelsea, still clad in the pink denim jacket and pants. If anything, she looked even more bowed down and miserable than she had that morning. It was as if the sun rose in the sky by means of levering its weight against her slim shoulders.

"Cheer up, Chelsea," Meg heard herself call out. "He'll be back soon enough."

The girl stared at her with such a mixture of shock and chagrin that Meg quickly added, "Your dad. I overheard you guys this morning. He's coming home for dinner, right?"

Chelsea was taken aback. Apparently, the possibility that someone might talk to her was a thought that had never crossed her mind. "He works a lot," she said finally. "You can never be sure when he might get done."

"It's a total yawn to be stuck here on your own all day," Meg agreed. "I mean, there are worse places. But still — how do you pass the time?"

"I — I have to go," the girl said stiffly. She rushed back into the elevator and let the doors swallow her up.

Meg frowned at the gleaming brass of the old-fashioned dial. Chelsea got off at the ninth floor. Meg could have sworn that she'd just come down from six.

Well, maybe that answers my question, she reflected. *She's so bored that she spends her days riding the elevators and wandering around the Royal Bostonian.*

A few minutes later, she tested her theory on Aiden, who had just returned from his day on the work crew.

He was suspicious. "Sounds fishy to me. Why would her father bring her on a business trip just to sit in the hotel?"

"It only sounds fishy because that's *our* story," Meg pointed out. "At least her father is a real person. Let's hope nobody starts wondering why they never see Louise Graham."

"You're right," said Aiden. "Still — if this girl stands out enough for you to notice her, then you probably stand out enough for somebody else to notice you. Tomorrow, when I'm at work, you should lie low somewhere."

"Aw, Aiden," Meg groaned. "Mom and Dad are in prison, and you've got me lounging around like some rich old lady who lives with her cats. There must be something I can do to help."

"Until we see Jane Macintosh on Monday, all we can do is to keep from getting caught. Nobody's ever going to find me pushing a lawn mower through some Brookline backyard. And you" — a smile slowly took hold of his normally serious features — "someplace dark, where all anybody ever sees is the back of your head."

"Don't talk in riddles," Meg said irritably. "I'm not in the mood."

"Go see a movie."

9

The trial.

Aiden dreamed about it often. He hadn't been in the courtroom for the whole thing, but it sure felt that way. He had read enough press coverage and studied enough transcripts for his mind to cobble together a complete and vivid memory of those five terrible months.

Most of it was almost, but not quite, boring enough to numb the horror of what was happening. *Endless* lawyer talk. Motions, objections, and sidebars — all as exciting as reading the telephone book out loud.

Then one day Dr. John Falconer's confident "Of course we'll be found innocent" had become "Of course we *are* innocent."

Even now, a year later, Aiden took it like a sucker punch to the gut. Something had changed — and not for the better.

"And the jury knows it, right?" Meg had asked.

Mom's reply: "No matter what happens, we'll never stop loving you."

Aiden had seen it then. Not Meg — not yet. But at that moment, the unthinkable had become thinkable. The "trial of the new millennium" would not go well for their parents.

In the end, it had come down to the Falconers' word against the will and might of the United States government. The secretary of Homeland Security himself took the stand against them. And that nine-foot FBI agent — Harris, the one who'd arrested the Falconers in the first place. Without Frank Lindenauer, there had been no way to refute the charges — no proof that the husband and wife criminologists had been working for the CIA all along.

The defense had presented witnesses — mostly Uncle Frank's many ex-girlfriends. The "aunts" — Aunt Trudy, Aunt Rachel, Aunt Essie, Aunt Ursula. The strategy had backfired. The testimony proved that the Falconers knew a man who called himself Frank Lindenauer, but little else. None of the girlfriends realized he was with the CIA. Not only had he kept his career secret, but each "aunt" believed Lindenauer was in a different line of work. Depending on which ex was on the stand, he was an architect, a massage therapist, an editor at *Mad* magazine, and the leader of a crew that put out oil well fires.

Soon these "jobs" were greeted by laughter in the courtroom. TV talk show hosts made top-ten lists about them. For Aiden, that was the cruelest part. The destruction of their family had already become a kind of reality show. Now it was turning into a sitcom as well.

There was certainly nothing funny about the verdict: guilty on all counts. And sentencing — Aiden didn't have to imagine that. He and Meg had both been there. The defense lawyers had felt the Falconer children might elicit sympathy from the judge.

There had been none.

Life behind bars.

Life.

Strange name for a prison sentence, Aiden had thought at the time. They called it life, but it was really the opposite of that. More like the end of life. The end of a comfortable, loving home; cracking jokes around the dinner table; Monopoly games fought to the death; making fun of the drugstore detective novels Dad wrote for fun.

The end of a family.

There had been total chaos in the courtroom.

Reporters scrambled for cell phones and Palm Pilots. A media feeding frenzy in full swing.

And for the Falconers and their two children — disbelief, tears, and, worst of all —

Time to say good-bye.

No! It's too awful to remember! No one should have to carry something like this around in his mind.

The pain was so sharp, the images so vivid. He could hear the excited voices, the running feet, the police sirens —

Wait a minute — there weren't any sirens at the trial. . . .

He sat bolt upright in the canopy bed, chest heaving, his face streaked with tears. The courtroom was gone, but —

"Sirens!" he whispered. They were wailing in the street below. The colored glow of flashing lights danced across the walls of the Provincetown Suite.

Barely keeping his panic under control, he dashed into the other bedroom and shook his sleeping sister by the shoulders. "Meg!"

"You're a dead man if you're still there when I open my eyes," she murmured without stirring.

"Cops!"

Fifty alarm clocks could not have provided a more total wake-up call. Meg bounded out of bed as if juiced with high voltage, flinging the heavy down comforter halfway across the room. *"Here?"*

"Outside." He flattened himself to the wall and peered down through the window. "In front of the building."

"Do you think they traced the frequent-flyer miles?" asked Meg, scrambling into her new jeans.

Aiden dismissed this with a wave of his hand. Another lesson from Fugitive 101: Worrying about the past was wasted energy. There was only the *now* — the next minute, the next move. "They'll be watching the elevators," he mused, pulling on pants and a shirt. "Probably the stairs, too."

"What about the window?" suggested Meg. "We can tie blankets together and climb down."

"Too risky. If they spot us, we'll be hanging there like ripe fruit." He frowned. There had to be some way.

The answer came from the craziest possible source — Mac Mulvey, the main character of Dad's detective novels. The books were filled with heart-pounding, rapid-fire action that bordered on unbelievable. Yet Mulvey's wild stunts had saved Aiden and Meg more than once since their flight from Sunnydale.

Over the years, Dr. John Falconer had plotted his

hero into dozens of deadly traps. Aiden racked his brains. Had Mulvey ever found himself cornered in a building, surrounded by enemies?

"The See Newark and Die Incident!" he exclaimed.

"The *what*?" All at once, she stared at him. "We're surrounded by cops, and you're talking about Dad's book?"

"Remember the abandoned apartment house? Mulvey had the microfilm, but Corelli's goons were getting closer —"

"Aiden, get to the point!"

"Follow me." He took her hand and led her out of the suite. Dead ahead, a bell sounded, and a spit-shined leather shoe at the end of a navy blue uniform pant leg stepped off the elevator.

A cop!

They stopped on a dime and raced as one in the opposite direction. Aiden's heartbeat was a drum-roll. It had been close. Another step would have put them directly in the officer's line of vision.

Meg mouthed the words "Where are we going?" But Aiden didn't dare answer, not with the enemy right here on the fourth floor. He saw a sign — EM-PLOYEES ONLY — and blasted through the door, dragging Meg behind him. They plowed into a snarl of housekeeping trolleys and bellhop carts. Aiden scanned the cramped space desperately. The object of his search was something he had never seen before, and he wasn't quite certain what to look for.

In *The See Newark and Die Incident*, Mac Mulvey was trapped inside a condemned apartment house. The Royal Bostonian was a palace compared to that dump, but Aiden was betting that the grand old hotel, with its stone gargoyles and brass appointments, had been built around the same time.

Then he spotted it — a rectangular hole in the wall, covered by hanging canvas straps. That was how Mulvey had managed to get past Corelli's enforcers — straight down the laundry chute.

10

Meg stared at him. "You're kidding, right?"

He hoisted himself up to the opening. "If we get separated —"

As usual, it was a subject she was unwilling to discuss. "We won't," she interrupted, and shoved him over the edge.

Aiden had always pictured Mulvey coasting through the guts of the abandoned apartment house on something like a slide. But the Royal Bostonian's laundry chute was an empty shaft. He toppled out to find nothing but thin air beneath him. With a cry of shock, he dropped like a stone through blackness that was broken only by wisps of light from the floors he hurtled past.

"Aiden!" cried Meg's voice from above.

He tried to shout a warning but could not get his mouth to form real words. He could feel himself accelerating. Terminal velocity, they called it —

the top speed for a falling body about to strike the earth.

I'm going to be a grease spot in the hotel basement!

The necessity of saving his sister from the same fate wrenched the scream from his throat, allowing him to produce language. "Don't jump!"

The impact came a split second later, a slamming jolt he felt from the top of his head to the tips of his toes. There was a loud metallic crash, and the darkness was replaced by a supernova of brilliant color in his brain. It blanked out all sensation, all thought except one: *Is this how it feels when you die?*

Then, suddenly, the light was back. The world flipped violently and he was somersaulting down the slope of an open aluminum hopper. His arms flailed, but he could not grab hold of anything to stop his descent, or even slow it. With a cartwheel of his stomach, he felt the metal beneath him disappear, and he was free-falling again, bracing himself for the final crash.

Wump!

An enormous mountain of tangled bedclothes cushioned his landing. His momentum drove him deep into the pile of sheets and pillowcases. He managed to swim to the surface just in time to see a howling, thrashing form drop from the hopper, missing him by inches.

He burrowed back down into the mound of linens and came up with his wild-eyed sister. She glared at him. "If we survive this," she said, "I'm going to kill you!"

"Come on!" They crawled out of the laundry and stood panting amid the banks of industrial-strength washing machines and dryers. Compared to the sumptuous lobby and plush guest accommodations, the Royal Bostonian's basement reminded Aiden of visiting his parents in prison — airless heat, fluorescent lighting, concrete floors. With effort, he forced the thought from his mind and pulled Meg out of the laundry room.

As they navigated the long hall, the faint scent of garbage gradually gave way to a different odor — car exhaust, spilled oil, burned rubber.

"The garage!" he exclaimed.

Meg was worried. "Won't that be the first place the cops look?"

"It's the only way out of the basement," he insisted. "We've got to chance it."

Crouching low, they darted through the rows of vehicles, pausing under cover of the taller SUVs.

They were just about to make a break for the exit ramp when the screech of tires froze them in their tracks. Brilliant headlights played across the cement walls. The Falconers dove back behind a Volvo wagon.

A sleek convertible swung off the ramp and screeched to a halt. A uniformed valet hopped out and tossed the keys to his partner in the glass booth.

"It's over," he announced. "The cops just left."

The desk man yawned with disinterest. "What was it all about?"

"A couple of high-society types came home from the opera and found their room got hit. Third robbery this week."

Aiden and Meg were thunderstruck. It had never occurred to either one of them that the police were there for a reason that had nothing to do with the fugitive Falconers.

Silently, they slunk out of the garage and crept down the deserted basement hall.

"I can't believe we almost got killed — for nothing!" groaned Meg.

Aiden rubbed a bruise on the hip that had made harsh contact with the aluminum hopper. "I'll take that any day of the week," he said tremulously. "The cops aren't on to us. That's all that matters."

Meg hauled open the heavy door to the hotel stairwell. "I'm going back to bed. The next time you wake me up, the building had better be on fire."

The McAllister Maximum Security Correction Facility in Thomaston, Florida, was a concrete and steel wasteland. The three thousand inmates imprisoned there were serving long sentences and were required to check all hope at the gate along with their personal effects.

This was the place that was now home to Dr. John Falconer and would be for the rest of his natural life.

Dr. Louise Falconer, his wife, was incarcerated at a women's facility ten miles away. Although physically close, the couple might as well have been on separate planets. The outer walls of McAllister were two feet thick, the window bars reinforced with titanium. The property was surrounded by three perimeters of electrified fencing, topped with bales of razor wire. Overseeing all this were twelve guard towers, manned 24/7, fixed with machine guns.

On the 28th of August, John Falconer was removed from his cell and marched, shackled and under heavy guard, to a windowless meeting room in the heart of the complex. There he found his wife waiting for him.

It should have been a happy reunion. But for a couple who knew that their children were missing, it was instead a heart-stopping shock.

"What's wrong? What happened?" he demanded, twisting and turning as the irons were removed. "The kids — "

A very tall figure stepped out of a shadowed corner. "Nothing's happened," Agent Emmanuel Harris said quickly. "Not that we know of."

John wheeled to face the six-foot-seven FBI agent. "You! What are *you* doing here?"

"I've come for your help."

John snorted a bitter laugh. "The one advantage to being already convicted is that I don't have to talk to you anymore. I'm still a criminologist. I know my rights!"

"John, listen to what he has to say!" his wife pleaded.

He embraced her, and they clung together. "You don't have to talk to him, either."

"We both have to — for Aiden and Meg."

Harris eased his bulk into a chair. "You don't have to like me. In fact, I'd be pretty surprised if you did. But we can all agree that Aiden and Margaret shouldn't be out on the street."

"I guess that makes you look pretty bad, huh?" John sneered. "Outsmarted by a couple of kids?"

"They've been smart," Harris acknowledged. "And resourceful. But mostly, they've been lucky, and luck always runs out. It's time to bring them in before something terrible happens."

Louise Falconer's outrage bubbled to the surface. "They're not going to turn themselves in so you can put them on another prison farm with criminals and delinquents! Offer them a decent life and they'll co-operate."

Harris looked grim. "They won't. We interrogated the boy they escaped with, Miguel Reyes. According to him, your kids are on the run looking for evidence to prove your innocence. They won't surrender, even if we offer to put them up at Club Med."

The parents looked profoundly shocked.

"I can't believe it!" murmured Louise. "They think they're doing it for *us*!"

"There's more," said Harris evenly. "They're leaving a trail of stolen vehicles, breaking and entering, vagrancy, and petty theft behind them. Also, Juvenile Corrections is talking about charging them with arson. I can get all that dropped — today. But if they're out there much longer, sooner or later they're going to do something *nobody* can fix. In that case, a prison farm will be their future, not just their past."

The Falconers exchanged agonized glances.

"That's if they make it at all," Harris went on. "You know how we picked up the Reyes kid? He got shot. And your son and daughter were in the same house at the time. It's a tough world. The kind of people living in this place — there are plenty of them still on the outside. You hate me; that's fine. But you've got to help me help your kids."

When John Falconer spoke again, it was with the voice of utter defeat. "Okay. Just tell us what we have to do."

Sunday — twenty-four hours to Aunt Jane.

The waiting was the hardest part for Meg. Aiden was the lucky one. He could lose himself in the mindless tasks of mowing, trimming, and raking.

I'm going to go nuts, hanging around here all day, talking to myself and sweating out tomorrow.

A movie. That had been Aiden's suggestion. Like she could concentrate on entertainment when the family's whole future depended on the meeting with Jane Macintosh. Better to mope around the hotel.

On the other hand, there had been room robberies at the Royal Bostonian. There could be plainclothes detectives. Stuff like that got blamed on kids all the time. She was totally innocent, but the last thing she needed was adults snooping around. In the course of figuring out what she didn't do, they might stumble across what she did.

Okay. The movies.

She needed a newspaper — the film section. Then

again, who cared what she saw? And she didn't know Boston well enough to make head or tail of a theater address.

Better just to wander the streets until I see a marquee, she decided. *It's not like I'm in a hurry today.*

She stepped off the elevator into the lobby and spotted the girl right away. Chelsea, sunk into a leather armchair, looking twice as miserable as she had yesterday.

The thought came to Meg instantly. *She needs a movie more than I do.*

She marched over and plunked herself down on the sofa across from the sad girl. "Hey, Chelsea."

Chelsea looked startled, then wary. "Hi."

"How's it going? I'm Meg." She gave her real name without thinking, and decided it was the right thing to do. She was suddenly struck by a need to be with someone her own age on a true and equal footing. Friendship was a luxury fugitives couldn't afford. But that didn't mean she and Chelsea couldn't be friends for one afternoon. Besides, if she called herself Belinda one more time, she was going to forget who she really was.

Chelsea was silent, her eyes focused once again on the floor.

"This hotel is pretty posh," Meg went on, "but

there's not much to do. I was thinking of hitting a movie. Want to come?"

Chelsea regarded her as if Meg had just suggested they stow away on the space shuttle. "I'd better not," she said finally. "My dad wouldn't like it."

Meg shrugged. "He doesn't have to know. If he's out till dinner again, that's six hours from now. We could see *three* movies, and you'd still be back in time! Come on. Aren't you *bored*?"

Chelsea appeared hopeful for a moment. But then two large tears spilled from her eyes and rolled down her pale cheeks.

Meg was appalled. "Hey, what did I say? I know your dad's kind of strict, but — "

"That's not it!" Chelsea sobbed softly.

"Then what's wrong?" Meg persisted. "Listen, we've all got our problems. Me, too. But what really drives you nuts is when you're cooped up all day with nothing to do but think about them. Let's get out of here, Chelsea."

Chelsea didn't say yes; she didn't even nod. But allowing Meg to haul her out of the lobby and onto the street was consent enough.

It was amazing how freedom from the Royal Bostonian seemed to remove a thousand-pound weight from around Chelsea's neck. Her step lightened; her posture straightened; her entire face was transformed. It would have been exaggerating to say she smiled, but she seemed to face the world with something other than gloom and dread.

Maybe it's because I don't ask too many nosy questions, Meg mused. *How can I? If I mind her business, she might want to mind mine.*

Whatever the reason, Chelsea was relaxing, and Meg found herself loosening up, too. They found a movie theater after about twenty minutes of wandering. Meg bought her ticket with Aiden's hard-earned cash, then hesitated. Should she pay for Chelsea as well? Just because the girl was wealthy didn't mean her father kept her flush with spending money.

She needn't have worried. Chelsea reached into her pocket and pulled out a wad of bills three inches thick. She peeled off a twenty and crammed the rest back out of sight.

Meg was bug-eyed. "Your dad lets you carry that much money? You'd better be careful. Some people in the hotel got robbed last night."

Chelsea looked shocked, then terrified and close to tears.

Meg was instantly contrite. "Sorry. I didn't mean

to scare you. I'm sure you guys know what you're doing. Let's just see the show, okay?"

But the damage was done. Meg could almost see the shutters coming down behind the girl's eyes. As a potential friend, Chelsea was closed for business.

It was the movie that saved the day, not because it was good, but because it was so bad that it was hilarious. The two girls sat in the front row, stifling screams and desperately trying not to choke on their popcorn.

Afterward, they reenacted the hokey chase scene along the streets of downtown Boston, pursuing each other with melodramatic intensity and peals of laughter. At one point, Chelsea darted through a troop of Cub Scouts, hurdling the string they all held to keep the group together, and disappeared into an alley. By the time Meg pounded onto the scene, the alley was deserted, and Chelsea was waving down at her from a fifth-floor fire escape.

Meg gawked up at her. "What are you — a monkey? Or a trapeze artist?"

Even from forty feet below, Meg could see Chelsea's expression change as the girl shut down once again. Even in fun, she couldn't handle any personal remarks.

This time, the change was permanent. The two returned to the hotel in uncomfortable silence.

Things went from bad to worse when they hit the lobby. For there, pacing up and down in a cold fury, was Chelsea's father.

He took hold of his daughter by the shoulders. "Are you out of your mind? I told you exactly what was expected of you today! And none of it included stepping out that door!"

Meg took a protective step forward. He was almost shaking the poor girl, getting right in her face, bullying and threatening. Chelsea was crying. It was obvious she was terrified of the man.

And suddenly Meg turned away, realizing she'd been on the verge of making a serious mistake. Even if speaking up for Chelsea was the right thing to do, Meg had greater responsibilities — to Aiden, and what the two of them were trying to accomplish; to Mom and Dad and the future of the Falconer family. Nothing was worth risking getting caught.

She slunk off to the elevator without a backward glance, reflecting that, yes, Chelsea was pretty weird. And no wonder.

12

Aiden and Meg stood on the sidewalk, gazing across East University Street at the glass and gunmetal mini-mall that housed Arrow Travel. They had been there for close to an hour already, trying to work up the courage to go inside.

Aiden was part embarrassed and part bewildered by the paralyzing fear that turned his legs to jelly. A fugitive lived with fear every moment of every day. They had been chased by police and Juvenile authorities and set upon by a mysterious attacker who seemed to be out to kill them. What was so frightening about approaching a travel agent?

Maybe it was this: If the meeting failed, if Jane Macintosh couldn't help them find Frank Lindenauer, then the Falconer kids would be nowhere, with all their bridges burned. There could be no next move, no plan B, no alternative trail to follow. It would be the end of all hope for Mom and Dad.

Meg shot him a nervous smile. "You could always go back to cutting lawns."

She had a knack for knowing what was eating him, and he was grateful to her for breaking the silence. "No, thanks." He swallowed hard. "I guess we'd better get this done."

It was ten to nine, the tail end of rush hour, and the streets were crowded. But the mini-mall, with its cracked terrazzo and dingy storefronts, was mostly deserted. Things became even quieter as they walked down the stalled escalator to the basement level and Arrow Travel.

"Good morning, kids. How can I help you?"

Aiden was battered by disappointment. The woman behind the desk was a complete and total stranger. She bore absolutely no resemblance to the Aunt Jane of Aiden's memory or to the young woman in the crinkled photograph in his pocket.

In a shaky voice he barely recognized as his own, he said, "Jane Macintosh?"

She looked surprised. "Do I know you?"

Wordlessly, Aiden pulled out the picture of Aunt Jane and Uncle Frank reclining in lounge chairs around the pool at the Red Jacket Motor Lodge in Colchester, Vermont. He held it for her and stood there, waiting, scarcely daring to breathe. He was barely aware of it when Meg's small hand stole into his.

It's a lost cause. She isn't the person in the picture. She's fatter. And blond, instead of brunette. We got it wrong! We made a mistake somewhere.

With a series of nearly audible clicks, Jane Macintosh recognized her younger self and her then-boyfriend. She remembered the vacation and the young family she had spent it with. And from that point, she took a guess at who might be coming to her with this piece of her history.

"Oh, my God!" She gawked at the two young people in her office. "You're not — the *Falconer* kids? Aiden?" She turned to the girl, who had been just a baby nine years ago. "Meg?"

The relief that flooded over Aiden was like the bursting of a dam. The emotion was too much for him to handle. There were no tears, but he was incapable of speech.

Aunt Jane ran out from behind her desk and pulled the brother and sister into her arms. "I can't imagine what you've both been through!" she exclaimed in a choked voice. "I watched the trial! I can't believe what your parents are accused of!"

"None of it's true!" said Meg stoutly.

"And what they said about Frank — "

Aiden found his voice at last. *"Where's* Frank? Why didn't he come forward during the trial?"

"Sweetheart, I don't know," Aunt Jane replied. "I haven't seen him for almost as long as I haven't seen you. We were only together for a few months. I'd barely thought about him until your poor parents started making the news."

"Did you know he was a CIA agent?" Aiden asked.

"That's why I never got in touch with your parents' lawyers," Aunt Jane explained. "I couldn't have helped their case. Frank told me he was some kind of art dealer. That's why he traveled so much."

"That was his cover!" Meg reasoned. "The other girlfriends all thought stuff like that, too."

Aunt Jane shrugged helplessly. "You might be right. But I can't help you find him. I don't know anything about the man. I can't even tell you if he's still alive."

Here it was, the dead end Aiden had feared all along. And yet he felt no panic, no despair, only a calm determination.

"Aunt Jane," he began, "we escaped from a prison farm in Nebraska. We were almost murdered by a psycho in Vermont. We're wanted by every cop and Juvenile officer in the country. We tracked you down from nine-year-old records in a motel that's located two thousand miles away from where we started out. The fact is — we've got nowhere to go after this. You *have* to help us!"

She looked genuinely distressed. "But I told you! I would if I could."

"Just talk to us," Aiden pleaded. "Talk about Frank Lindenauer. You might remember something new, or a detail that you don't think is important but might ring a bell with us."

"I'll try. I really will." She sat them down in the office's small waiting area — two folding chairs in front of a closed-captioned TV set tuned to CNN. She perched on the edge of her desk.

"I met Frank in ski school, of all places. We were both learning to snowboard. By the end of the weekend, we were an item. Everything was fast with Frank. He was a fast talker; he walked like he was being chased — I had to scramble to keep up with him on the sidewalk. He made a lot of money and spent it before it ever hit his pocket. He had this old BMW that he'd brought over from Germany, where there's no speed limit. He had that car up to a hundred and forty on the Mass Pike! I was screaming in his ear to slow down, but he just laughed. That's part of the reason we broke up. I honestly thought he was going to get me killed! He was *always* a crazy driver."

"What was he like?" Meg persisted. "Was he a nice person? Was he good to you?"

"In his way, I suppose. He was charming, the life of every party. And I was nuts about him. He was just hard to pin down."

"Because he was a CIA agent," Aiden said with a nod.

"I don't know," she mumbled. "I never believed that CIA stuff when it came up during the trial. But now that I think about it, there was plenty that pointed to Frank being more than he seemed. There were a lot of girls like me, and he told each of us he was in a different line of work.

"Another thing — in all the time I knew him, he threw cash around like it was free. He never once paid for anything with a credit card. I figured he was just paranoid about someone stealing the number. But when you think about it, a credit card is something that can be traced."

The telephone rang, but she let an answering machine pick it up. "Listen, kids, I've been away for a few days, so I really have to get back to my clients. But I promise I won't let you down. After work, let's all three of us go to the police. I'll tell them everything I know about Frank. If there's anything to find, they're the people who are trained to find it."

"No chance!" said Meg stubbornly. "They don't want the truth. They just want to keep Mom and Dad in jail forever!"

"You have to understand, Aunt Jane," Aiden explained. "We can't trust the authorities. Nobody knows why Frank Lindenauer didn't come forward to support Mom and Dad at the trial. But one of the reasons might be that the government wouldn't let him. Remember, the CIA refused to admit that they even had an agent by that name."

"But you're just kids," she pleaded. "This is too much for you to handle on your own."

"We made it this far," Meg said, her jaw set.

Aunt Jane wasn't giving up. "But what if I tell them — "

"All you have is an opinion," Aiden cut her off. "For the government to open a closed case, something big has to happen. We can't go to the police until we find Frank Lindenauer and bring him along with us. Otherwise, they'll just throw us back into juvenile detention. And then no one will be looking for the truth."

The telephone rang again, and once more Aunt Jane made no move for it. Aiden could see she was thinking it over. At last, she scribbled an address on a Post-it note and handed it to him.

"I'll help you if I can, but there's one condition. You have to come and stay with me. I can't have you living on the street."

Aiden stifled a grin, thinking of their luxury suite at the five-star Royal Bostonian.

"I should be home by six," she continued. "Take a taxi. Do you need money?"

Aiden shook his head. "I've been working. But are you sure you want us in your house? I mean, talking to us is one thing. But isn't it a crime to harbor fugitives?"

She gave him a watery smile. "Your mom and dad didn't know me from a hole in the ground, but they were lovely to me on that Vermont trip. My biggest worry is that I might not be able to help you." She escorted them to the door. "I'll see you at six. We'll order pizza or something."

"Thanks, Aunt Jane," said Aiden. And he truly meant it. Nothing was solved, and still might never be. But just the idea that someone was on their side made him feel a lot less alone.

They were just about to exit Arrow Travel when the door of the next office opened, and out stepped an impeccably dressed fortyish man carrying a leather briefcase. The Falconers were so used to being anonymous strangers in this city that it took a moment for Meg to realize that she recognized this person.

It was Chelsea's father.

She turned to Aunt Jane. "Next door — that's a pawnshop, right?"

The travel agent made a face. "I suppose you could call it that. I'm pretty sure it's a front for fencing stolen goods. This complex has really gone downhill. I've got to find some new office space."

Once out in the mini-mall, Meg shared her discovery with Aiden.

"So what?" he said, preoccupied. "So he visits a pawnshop. Maybe he's not as rich as you think he is."

"Don't you get it?" she persisted, annoyed that he didn't share her excitement. "I told you how Chelsea bought a movie ticket with a wad of bills that would choke a hippo! And she climbed that fire escape like the Human Fly! She's the hotel burglar! Her father makes her rob people's rooms, and then he comes here to sell the stuff!"

Aiden looked at her with respect. "You're probably right, Meg. Now we know who to thank for our trip down the laundry chute."

Meg was outraged. "Is that all it means to you? That complete jerk is forcing his daughter into a life of crime!"

"How do you know he's forcing her?"

"Are you kidding? The girl is totally miserable! She cries every time the wind blows! She's *definitely* a victim. Now, what are we going to do about it?"

Aiden looked her straight in the eye. "I'll tell you what we're going to do about it. We're going to go back to the hotel, pack up our stuff, and get out of there before she works her way up to *our* room!"

"Come on!" his sister countered. "All we have to do is tip off the cops. Nothing'll happen to Chelsea once they realize her father's making her do it."

Aiden groaned in frustration. "You can't be serious! We have to steer clear of cops, no matter what! How would you feel if we lost our chance to help Mom and Dad over something like this?"

She was chastened. "Okay. I just feel bad for her, that's all. It's frustrating to know you can help somebody, but you don't dare try it."

Aiden had another argument. "I don't think we of all people should have anything to do with putting someone else's father in jail."

"This is different," Meg insisted. "The guy deserves it. He's a bully and a jerk." A raindrop splashed off the tip of her nose.

The two ducked into a bus shelter just before a heavy cloudburst deluged the street. When a downtown bus happened along a few minutes later, it seemed natural to hop aboard and ride it back to the Royal Bostonian.

Meg sat in listless silence, watching the rain stream down the grimy window. *Can't help Chelsea,* she thought. *We'll find out tonight if we can help Mom and Dad.*

And suddenly, Mom and Dad were directly in her line of vision.

13

Meg goggled. *Twenty* Moms and Dads, as a matter of fact.

She was on her feet in a split second, slapping repeatedly at the signal to request a stop.

"Meg, what are you doing?" hissed a bewildered Aiden.

The bus driver glanced back to see who was ringing the bell over and over again. "I heard you the first time, kid."

Meg continued to hit the bell. "Stop the bus! It's an emergency!"

The bus lurched to a halt, and Meg hauled Aiden out into the rain.

"What's with you?" he complained. "We're getting drenched!"

"Look!" she shrieked.

In the display window of TV Town, two dozen monitors, large and small, angled and flat, regular and high definition, were all tuned to the same channel. The screens showed Drs. John and Louise Falconer, dressed alike in orange jumpsuits, seated at a bare table.

Aiden and Meg pushed their way through the crowd of people huddled from the rain in the recessed doorway of the store.

The voice of their father reached them like a homing signal the instant they burst inside.

". . . we see what you're doing. We understand it, and we love you for it. But it's over. It's time to give yourselves up."

Aiden and Meg stared at each other, unable to believe their ears.

Then the camera focused on their mother, who looked thin and sleep deprived. "This is what we want you to do. Your future matters more than anything that's happening to us. Our problems aren't as important as your safety. Aiden, Meg, *please*! Find the nearest police station and turn yourselves in."

The camera panned, and Aiden and Meg realized that, sitting beside their parents, was the hated FBI agent, Emmanuel Harris.

"Look who's with them!" hissed Meg in a rage.

"Kids," said Harris into the camera, "listen to

your parents. They want what's best for you. *Everyone* wants what's best for you. All the laws that have been broken up to now — we can work that out. You have my personal guarantee that you'll be treated fairly."

"Lousy traitors!" snarled a man standing close by them in the store. "They should have fried the both of them, and their rotten kids, too!"

The CNN anchor returned to the screen. *"You've been watching a dramatic plea from convicted traitors John and Louise Falconer, reaching out to their runaway children to give themselves up."*

Then, shockingly, the screen filled with still images of Aiden and Meg — the mug shots from their arrival at Sunnydale Farm.

Observation #1: They looked very different now. Most of this was on purpose. Meg's long hair was cut short and bleached blond. Aiden, who was fairer, had dyed his hair jet-black. The kids were thinner, too, and stress and hardship had etched worry lines into their faces. The pictures were eight months old, but the people in them appeared at least two years younger.

Observation #2 (much scarier): They were still all too recognizable, especially in a crowd of shoppers looking at the Sunnydale photographs projected onto a sixty-inch plasma screen.

"Oh, my God!" A frail elderly woman stood gawking at them. "It's *you*! You're those kids!"

The message flashed between brother and sister at tachyon speed: *Run!*

By the time heads turned to follow the woman's pointing finger, the Falconers were twin blurs blasting out through the crowd still huddling in the doorway. The blowing rain drenched them as they tore along the sidewalk.

With a sinking heart, Aiden realized that, because of the weather, they were virtually the only pedestrians on the street. If anyone heeded the old lady's warning, the Falconers would be as difficult to spot as a pair of polar bears.

Of course, it worked two ways. If somebody was after them, that would be obvious, too.

Aiden risked a backward glance. "Nobody's chasing us!"

"Yeah!" puffed Meg. "Because they're all on the phone to the cops!" She steered him through a narrow alley, and they pounded down cement stairs to an underground T-station. They boarded the first train that came along, without knowing where it was headed. As long as it put distance between them and TV Town, it had to be the right direction.

Meg shivered in her wet clothes and tried to sink into her seat. "Is it just me," she whispered, "or is everybody looking at us?"

"I think it's only because we're soaked," Aiden murmured back.

"What are we going to *do*?" she persisted. "Our pictures were just on national TV! That woman recognized us! Other people will, too."

Aiden tried to be big brotherly, but it was clear that he was also badly shaken. "Take it easy."

But in spite of all assurances, Meg understood that the rules of this cruel game had changed once again. They were now exposed. From this moment on, the enemy could be anyone with a sharp eye, a good memory, and a TV set.

In the small office of Arrow Travel, Jane Macintosh reached for a tissue and blew her nose. Her eyes were still glued to the television in her waiting area, where the couple she had vacationed with nine years before had just issued an emotional plea to their fugitive children.

The same children she'd just agreed to harbor and help. Barely an hour had passed since they'd left her office. It had seemed so sensible then — so much the right course of action.

But now, with their distraught parents begging for their safety, keeping them out in the world, with danger all around them, felt like the worst kind of madness.

What on earth was she going to do?

14

Five o'clock found the Falconers in the back row of the darkened planetarium, watching a red giant star go supernova for the fourth time.

"If that thing explodes once more," Meg murmured, "my head is going with it."

But Aiden had insisted that this was the best place to be on the day that their faces had been telecast to millions. Here it was dark, and people were looking up instead of at one another. There were a lot of kids around, too — field trips and day camps — so two more just blended into the scenery.

The decision had been made hours earlier that the Royal Bostonian was history for them. It was just too risky to return to a place where their faces were known, and any desk clerk or bellhop might have been watching CNN that morning.

"I give us twelve hours before we start stinking again," Meg predicted darkly. "Those extra clothes were all we owned in this world."

"What are you complaining about?" Aiden mumbled. "I cut a million acres of grass to earn the money for that stuff. And I've got the blisters to prove it."

"In a way we were lucky," Meg decided. "If we'd missed that broadcast, we'd have had no idea that our pictures were on national TV — not until the cops grabbed us up."

Sitting beside her in the dim light, chilled by damp clothes and too much air-conditioning, Aiden shivered. "That's what Mom and Dad said they want — us with the cops, I mean."

She shrugged it off. "What did you expect them to say with J. Edgar Giraffe in there with them? I never thought I'd have to look at his ugly face again!"

Oh, how Aiden envied Meg's view of life! In her eleven-year-old world, everything was black and white, and her loyalty was absolute. For Aiden, nothing was ever so straightforward.

"They looked sincere to me, and also pretty upset about us," he mused. "All that stuff about our safety being more important than anything — you've got to admit that sounds like something they'd say."

She stared at him. "What are you talking about? They don't want us to give ourselves up! We're their only hope! Without us, who's going to prove they're innocent?"

Aiden was silent. It was something he would never mention to his sister, a thought so awful that he felt like a monster for even allowing it to cross his mind: What if they *weren't* innocent? What if John and Louise Falconer had been found guilty because they *were* guilty?

What are you — crazy? This is Mom and Dad! Of course they're innocent!

And yet the nagging doubt would not leave him: What if Mom and Dad wanted their kids to stop looking for the evidence that would prove their innocence because there was nothing to find?

No-o-o-o-o!!!

Meg was regarding him with alarm. "Wait a minute — you're not seriously thinking about turning ourselves in?"

Aiden straightened his back and set his jaw. "No, I'm not." He checked the luminous dial of his watch. "Come on. It's time to go to Aunt Jane's."

All the way in the taxi, Aiden watched the rear-view mirror and the darting eyes of the driver. Was he checking the traffic or his two passengers, who perhaps looked familiar?

Does it count as being paranoid if everyone really is out to get you?

Aunt Jane's apartment was in nearby Brookline. Aiden had worked at a dozen buildings just like this one in his three days with the lawn crew — low-rise redbrick apartment houses on well-kept tree-filled properties.

Meg pressed the buzzer marked 3C, MACINTOSH, and they started up in the elevator.

Aiden could tell that something had changed the instant Aunt Jane opened her door. Her expression was somehow wrong. Sad. Even — *guilty?*

And then he saw, standing in the hallway behind her, a man in a blue uniform shirt with a gold badge on the pocket.

"Meg — *run!*"

He was amazed at how fast the cop burst into action behind Aunt Jane. It was like he'd been fired from a cannon.

Meg scrambled down the steps, Aiden hot on her heels.

Aunt Jane was crying now, her sobs echoing in the stairwell: "Please forgive me! This is what your parents want for you! I'm so sorry!"

Meg hit the second-floor landing and wheeled to

take the next flight. An instant later, Aiden hurled himself around the banister. Through the corner of his eye, he saw that the cop was only a few steps behind him.

"Give it up, kid!" the officer puffed.

It lent Aiden's feet wings.

All at once, he heard his sister gasp. She stopped so suddenly that he bumped into her, sending her sprawling headlong.

"Meg!"

Her forward momentum propelled her out and away from the stairs, and he could only watch in horror, unable to reach her. She was about to fly to a terrible crash at the bottom.

And then he was there, the figure who had made her freeze — a second cop starting up from the ground floor. Miraculously, he caught her and held on, the officer and his fleeing felon. Rescue and capture in a single instant.

Aiden hesitated.

His sister did not. "Go!" Anyone else would have been too shaken to think. But not Meg Falconer. "It's all on you now!"

A hand from behind clamped hard onto Aiden's shoulder.

He twisted free, scrambling over the banister and

dropping to the lobby floor. He was outside in a flash, pounding down the sidewalk, relieved to see there was no more police presence.

The last thing he heard before the heavy door swung shut was his sister's firm voice: "If you come back for me, I'll break every bone in your body!"

15

Aiden had never run so far or so fast in his life. Propelled by his sister's words as much as fear of pursuit, he put one foot in front of the other and repeated the process with no regard to aching legs or burning lungs.

On the next block, he passed a parked squad car and took note of the markings: TWELFTH PRECINCT. In spite of everything, he couldn't bring himself to feel anger toward the Brookline police. One of their officers had probably saved Meg from a broken neck.

Meg.

The reality began to sink in. His proud, spirited little sister was in custody. Amid all the terrible things that had happened to Mom and Dad and the Falconer family, the one bright spot had always been that he was with Meg.

Now that was gone, too.

He forced the lump out of his throat. It was slowing him down.

The handcuffs were on the loosest possible setting, but the metal still grabbed her flesh. When Officer Jankowski finally uncuffed her in the small interrogation room, it took a lot of rubbing to get the circulation back in her wrists.

"Sorry, kid," Jankowski told her. "Procedure."

Meg said nothing. The experience of her parents had given the entire family an intense mistrust of the judicial system.

"Your brother — he must be a track star or something. We've got a lot of personnel in that neighborhood, but he's gone with the wind."

She had resolved to give the police no response whatsoever, but her pride was hard to suppress.

"You see, you're not supposed to be smiling," Jankowski chided. "Your brother — he'd be a lot better off if he was in here with you, safe and sound. You'd be doing him a big favor if you'd just tell us where to find him."

"I don't know where he is."

"Fair enough. So what's your best guess? Any

favorite haunts? Friends in town he might reach out to?"

"Yeah, one," said Meg bitterly. "She sold us out to the cops."

"Listen." Officer Jankowski was growing a little less patient. "I know this may be hard for you to accept, but we're the good guys. Whatever you kids have done in other places, you're squeaky clean in the Commonwealth of Massachusetts."

Meg pounced on this. "I'm not under arrest?"

"You're in protective custody. We're holding you until a gentleman from Washington, DC, can come and pick you up."

Meg felt her blood run cold. A gentleman from DC.

Did Jankowski mean J. Edgar Giraffe himself, Agent Emmanuel Harris?

If so, Meg was about to be handed over to the man who had destroyed the Falconer family.

Agent Harris was in Starbucks, in search of the only decent coffee in Thomaston, Florida, when the call came through on his cell phone. One of the two Falconer kids, the daughter, was in police custody in Brookline, Massachusetts.

"What about the boy?" he demanded. "Aiden?

Do they have a line on him? Those two stick together. He can't be far away."

"It looks like he gave them the slip," his Washington assistant reported. "They've been pounding the pavement for four hours, but no luck."

Harris almost choked. "They've had her for *four hours*, and you're telling me *now*?"

"They just let us in the loop," came the reply. "The official notification went to Juvenile Corrections."

"Juvenile Corrections?" Harris barked in the face of the stunned baristo, who was holding out his triple espresso. "Those are the nitwits who came up with the brainstorm to put two innocent kids on a prison farm!"

He took note of a wounded air in his assistant's tone. "So will you be flying up there tonight?"

Harris checked his watch and snorted in disgust. "I would have, if somebody had told me four hours ago. It's too late to make the last flight now." He snatched up his coffee and downed half of it in a single gulp. "Tell them I'll be on the first plane tomorrow."

Lieutenant Helen Tannahill was the third-watch commander at the twelfth precinct in Brookline.

Coming on shift at midnight, she was used to walking in on all sorts of work in progress. So she wasn't surprised when she glanced through the one-way glass into interrogation room 3 and saw a young girl, her head on the table, fast asleep.

She looked questioningly at a passing officer. "Runaway?"

"You could say that," the man replied. "That's one of the Falconer kids — you know, the parents got life."

Now the lieutenant was surprised. "Yeah? How did *we* end up with her?"

"They had a family friend in town. Tipped us off. With friends like that, huh?"

"Wasn't there a brother?" the lieutenant asked.

"He got away from us."

Tannahill groaned. "That'll read well in the papers."

The officer shrugged. "It's not our case, really. We're just holding her for federal Juvenile. They're picking her up in the morning."

The lieutenant glared at him. "And everybody here thought it was just fine to leave her there all night, falling asleep on her face?"

He looked embarrassed. "Aw, Helen, we couldn't put her in a cell. The kid's only eleven."

The lieutenant was disgusted. "Who thinks for you when I'm off duty? Take her up to the crash pad and lock her in from the outside. At least it has a cot."

"It's not regulation," the officer warned.

"Neither is she," Tannahill snapped. "Make her comfortable."

The flashlight was propped up on its base, casting a beam of yellowish light onto the corrugated aluminum ceiling of the tool shed. Aiden reclined amid the shovels and coiled hoses, chest still aching from his bruising run.

This prefab shed in the backyard of a split-level house was probably the only reason he wasn't in custody right now. Yesterday — was it truly only *yesterday?* — he had been part of the crew that was cutting this lawn. It had been pure luck that his flight had brought him onto Acorn Street and the unlocked garden shed he'd so recently trimmed around with the weed whacker.

He checked his watch. It was almost one A.M. He was pretty sure he was safe — for now. Realistically, the police wouldn't tear Brookline apart all night just to find him. That was the good news. And the bad news? He was nowhere, and that wasn't just a comment on his location. He had no place to go, nothing to do, no next move. Aunt Jane had been their only lead.

The betrayal stung almost as much as the cuts and scrapes that his mad dash through bushes and over fences had left on him. He didn't even blame Aunt Jane so much. All she had done was give in to the emotional TV plea from Mom and Dad. He had very nearly gone for it himself.

No, the worst part was this: Jane Macintosh had genuinely wanted to help them. If she could be convinced to turn them in, then he could never trust anyone, anywhere.

A chilling thought.

The reality that he was the only Falconer not in jail pressed down on him like the weight of the whole world. Meg had said it at her capture: "It's all on you now!" The future of this battered family rested on his narrow shoulders.

Well, he didn't want it. It was too much for him. No single person was strong enough to carry that burden.

Oh, come on! he thought in disgust. *Where's your backbone?*

The answer came to him in a moment of perfect

clarity: His backbone was being held at the twelfth precinct.

That was his next move — to rescue Meg before they broke her spirit.

Or before she breaks their police station, he thought with a twisted smile.

No, not funny, he reminded himself, shifting his weight on a sack of Weed-B-Gone. Sure, Meg was strong. But she was an eleven-year-old girl. Big city cops were used to handling murderers and thugs. Poor Meg didn't stand a chance.

You don't stand a chance, either.

It was true. Breaking someone out of a police station was the kind of thing Mac Mulvey did in Dad's books. But fiction wasn't real life. More than likely, he would not be Meg's rescuer. He would be her cell mate. This plan, he recalled, was exactly what she didn't want him to do.

Tough darts, Meg. I'm coming after you.

The flashlight burned out with a pop, and darkness fell all around him. He snuggled down into the sack of Weed-B-Gone and shut his eyes, hoping for the sleep he knew would never come.

16

The twelfth precinct had its own rush hour. It was the time each morning after the sun rose, revealing a whole new rash of overnight crimes. These always seemed to be reported around the eight A.M. shift change. That was when the main entrance to the station house became a churning sea of people — cops and civilians, victims and suspects, clerical and cleaning staff.

This probably explained why the desk sergeant took no notice of one young citizen who might have stood out at a less busy time of day. His khakis and polo shirt had come directly from the store; their packaging creases attested to that fact. His Red Sox baseball cap still bore the Major League Baseball holographic sticker. Most suspicious of all, his mustache did not quite match the color of the hair that stuck out from beneath the cap. Judging from the lack of beard shadow on his fair cheeks, it was an unlikely mustache altogether. In fact, if Aiden hadn't been so scared, he probably would have been blushing with embarrassment to be seen in a cheap joke-shop mustache he wouldn't have worn on April Fools' Day at school.

He looked like a dork, he admitted to himself. *But you don't wave your face around a police station when you're the kid they've been combing the whole city for.* A lousy disguise was better than no disguise at all.

He mumbled something about a stolen motorcycle and was directed to take a number and wait to file his report.

He found a seat in the last row of benches and hunkered down, making himself small. A few minutes later, he got up and edged his way to the men's room, which was located partway down an office-lined corridor.

As he scouted his surroundings, the enormity of the task he had set himself began to sink in. The precinct house was a big place, with winding halls and dead ends. If a noncop got caught wandering in the wrong section, that would arouse suspicion — especially a noncop with an eighty-nine-cent mustache. And there were three floors. How was he ever going to find Meg?

Instead of going into the bathroom, he turned left

down another hall. It was a decision he regretted instantly. For there, walking toward him, was the very same policeman who had chased him in Aunt Jane's apartment building fourteen hours before.

He felt the hair on the back of his neck bristling, and a paralyzing cold seized him. He could run, but to where? The anteroom was full of cops. He was caught! Caught before he'd ever really started.

The officer was ten feet away. Then five. Aiden felt the man's eyes on him, like twin lasers, searing through his skin. He was laid bare, fully exposed. He waited for the look of recognition that would signify the end of this foolhardy plan, Aiden's freedom, and any slim chance the Falconers may have had to reclaim their lives.

It didn't come. Instead, the officer gave him a disinterested glance and said, "Looking for Motor Vehicle Records? Down the hall on your left, room 110."

"Thanks," he managed in his deepest voice. His heart pounding as if he'd just completed a marathon, he continued along the corridor, past 104, 106 . . . anything to put some distance between him and this officer who, at any moment, might have a flash of memory.

Room 110. The sign read: ARCHIVES — MOTOR VEHICLES.

What are you doing here? he berated himself. *They aren't going to be holding Meg in a file room! That's all this is — records on fender benders and crazy drivers.*

He froze. An odd feeling came over him, one that told him there was something he should be paying attention to. Why did that sound so familiar?

Crazy drivers . . .

And then it came to him. According to Jane Macintosh, Frank Lindenauer was a crazy driver, addicted to fast cars and high speeds. That had been part of the reason for their breakup.

He stared at the endless rows of tall file cabinets that stretched practically to infinity. The idea was bouncing around his head with such velocity that he had to wait for it to slow down before he could process it. If Lindenauer was half the driving maniac Aunt Jane said he was, then surely he'd gotten some speeding tickets. Which meant he had a file right here in this room.

That file would have other information, too — like addresses and phone numbers that might hold the key to finding the guy!

The service counter was deserted, but Aiden

could hear the voices of two clerks somewhere in the stacks. His feet barely touching the floor, he advanced cautiously into the room. MOVING VIOLATIONS, the sign read. That would cover speeding. He took in the vast array of labeled drawers.

Driving in Brookline must be like playing bumper cars, he thought, scanning for the *L*'s.

The rolling sound as he pulled the drawer open was like thunder in his ears. But the clerks, wherever they were in the labyrinth, took no notice.

Landau — Lennon — Linden — the name blazed out at him like a neon sign: *Lindenauer, Francis X.*

He removed the manila folder. And froze.

His peripheral vision detected distant motion at the far end of the aisle created by the ranks of cabinets. He flattened himself against the drawers.

Had they seen him?

No. They're just passing back and forth as they work.

Not daring to breathe, he darted around to the cover provided by the end of the row. He took the sheaf of papers out of the file, folded it once, and jammed it under his shirt and into the waistband of his pants.

A sudden voice from the left, much closer than he expected, nearly propelled him out of his skin. The two clerks were in the very next aisle, moving his

way. The muscles tensed in Aiden's calves as he pre-
pared to spring for the exit.

Then he heard a word that froze him in his
tracks: Falconer.

" . . . they've got her up in the crash pad till Juvie
can come and get her."

"Why should she get the royal treatment?" said
the second voice.

"She's a little kid. Where do you want to put her
— in the lockup?"

"Lousy terrorists! It's no more than she deserves!"

Aiden heard the sound of drawers sliding open
and shut. He would never get a better chance than
this. He was off like a shot, swooping out of room
110. He sprinted up the hall and blasted through the
door of the men's room, sucking air.

With sheer relief came a wave of nausea, and he
stood over the sink, dry-heaving.

The crash pad! That was where they were holding Meg!

What the heck is a crash pad?

17

The Constables' Dayroom was a small office on the third floor, equipped with a folding cot and a tiny bathroom. It was normally used for minor first aid and for police personnel to grab a short nap between shifts. For this reason, it was seldom called by its real name. The staff of the twelfth precinct referred to it as the crash pad.

Today, however, the crash pad was serving as a holding cell for Meg Falconer. She'd been brought here, half asleep, in the middle of the night, and tucked in by somebody nice. This morning, she had woken up to find a toothbrush, toothpaste, washcloth, soap, and towel all neatly laid out in the bathroom.

But make no mistake about it, she thought darkly, *the door's locked from the outside, there's a steel security gate on the window, and I'm surrounded by cops. This is a jail.*

At least Aiden got away. She comforted herself

with the thought of her brother far from this place, maybe even en route to another city. In her mental picture, he was carrying on the crusade to prove their parents' innocence. He was Mom and Dad's only hope now.

And mine, too, she realized.

But in her heart she knew Aiden was almost as helpless as she was. Jane Macintosh had been their only clue. Sure, he was free to go on searching. But where?

Aiden's a smart guy. He'll figure it out.

Yes, but he could also be a pretty big wimp. Meg was reasonably sure her brother had toyed with the idea of turning them both in after their parents' plea on television. True, he could show real guts sometimes. But that usually came when he was doing something straight out of one of Dad's cheese-ball detective novels.

Oh, God, Aiden, please don't blow this!

Restless, she wandered to the window and peered down through the steel mesh into the parking lot. The feds were coming to get her this morning. The next car that pulled up to the station could very well have that jerk, Agent Harris, at the wheel. She snickered when a tiny subcompact putt-putted up the ramp. Well, this one wasn't him. A seven-foot ox like Harris couldn't fit his pinky toe into that motor-ized roller skate.

She watched the comings and goings for a while, sinking herself into a deep despair. As games went, Where's Harris? was not likely to put her into a good mood.

And then she saw him. Not Emmanuel Harris. That would have been bad enough. But this —

Out of a fire-engine-red Hummer H-2 stepped a large, muscular man with a bull neck and a com-pletely bald head.

Meg turned to stone at the window, recalling where she had seen this person before. A deserted lake house in Vermont; a desperate struggle in near darkness; shots ringing out in the night; a terrified flight from a madman with a gun . . .

This madman.

The light had been bad at their first meeting, but there was no question in her mind.

You never forget the face of someone who wants you dead.

She was looking at Hairless Joe.

She watched the assassin cross the parking lot to the station entrance, her mind working at lightning speed.

Hairless Joe here? Why?

It couldn't be a coincidence.

When someone tries to kill you in Colchester, Vermont, and tracks you down six days later in Brookline, Massachusetts, it's because he's hunting you.

Hairless Joe was here for her. Somehow he must have found out that she was in custody at the twelfth precinct. And he had come to finish the job.

I can't even run away! I'm a sitting duck!

She raced to the door and rattled the handle. *"Hey!"* she bellowed at top volume. "Help me! It's an emergency! You've got to let me out of here!"

No one answered.

With a sinking heart, she remembered from sleepy impressions of last night that her bedroom/prison was tucked away in a corner of the third floor, surrounded by storerooms and equipment closets.

"He's going to kill me!" she screamed, pounding on the door with her fists. "I'm not kidding around! I need protection!"

She hacked and kicked at the doorknob, to no avail. She pulled an old framed photograph off the wall and bashed the lock with it. The glass shattered, and the frame fell to pieces, but it had no effect on the handle. She was still trapped.

"Help! *Help!*"

Another thought came to her: If Hairless Joe had learned where she was, maybe he had friends here, or some kind of fake police ID. Then he'd have the run of the place. All her cries for help might only serve to lead him to her.

I'm completely out of options.

No. There was one more.

If she couldn't run away, she had to stand and fight.

18

It took everything Aiden had to work up the courage to leave the men's room. He had Meg's location —the crash pad, whatever that was. But there was also time pressure. The feds were coming for her that morning. Aiden had to reach her first.

This place is a rabbit warren, he thought in rising panic. *All the hallways look the same.*

He spied a stairwell up ahead. Should he go to the upper floors? Down to the basement?

It was risky. The farther he got from the main squad room, the harder it would be to explain why he was wandering through the precinct house.

And then he saw it: At the base of the stairs was a fire department map of the layout of the building, floor by floor, room by room.

Aiden ran to it, reading every caption, taking in every detail. Crash pad . . . crash pad . . .

Oh, come on, where's the crash pad?

He remembered from Dad's books that cops had nicknames for everything. The precinct was the "house," the criminal was the "perp," an arrest was a "collar." So what on this diagram could be a crash pad?

His eyes fell upon a small room in the east corner of the third floor. The icon that identified it was a stick figure lying on a small bed.

Crash pad! A place to crash!

A bedroom!

He took the stairs three at a time. Each step, he knew, drew him farther away from any believable explanation of what he was doing there.

No cops . . . so far, so good.

He rounded the second-floor landing to see an older woman on the way down. Not an officer — probably just a secretary. Aiden lowered his head and brushed right past her.

Third floor. According to the map, the crash pad was in the far corner of the building. He scouted the long hall. The coast was clear.

But if anybody sees me . . .

This was hostile territory, and he was a wanted man.

Left turn. Or was Meg being held off to the right?

All at once, he wasn't sure. Uncertainty swelled inside him, and with it came an icy panic.

Calm down. This is too important!

Mentally, he rotated the firefighter's map until the layout lined up with the array of corridors and doorways in front of him.

Left. Definitely left.

His heart was pounding in his ears. The crash pad was at the end of this hall. As he walked lightly past closed storerooms and deserted offices, he allowed himself to feel a faint surge of hope. The third floor had none of the buzz of activity and conversation that filled the rest of the building.

Maybe — just maybe — he was going to reach his sister.

Aiden stopped in front of the last door. CONSTABLES' DAYROOM, it was marked. Aiden tried the knob.

Locked — *oh, no!* Wait, it was locked from *this* side! He twisted the bolt until there was a click, and the door swung wide.

In an instant, Aiden took in the small room with the folding cot. It was deserted. He peered into the bathroom. Empty.

Desperately, he looked around. *Have they already come to get her? Am I too late?*

And then his eyes fell on the closet.

Meg crouched behind some hanging uniforms. Fear had sharpened her ears into precision instruments. Someone was in the crash pad — his clumsy, hurried movements rattled around her hypersensitive brain.

Hairless Joe.

He was only a few feet away from her.

She heard the jiggle of a hand on the doorknob.

This is it!

Channeling years of gymnastics training into a single move, Meg grabbed hold of the hanging bar, swung back, and slammed both feet into the closet door with battering-ram force. It jolted open, smacking Aiden right in the nose. He staggered back and crumpled to the ground, whacking his head on the metal side of the cot.

Meg was on him in an instant, brandishing a spike of broken glass from the picture frame. With a battle cry, she brought it to the throat of her enemy, her stalker, her . . .

. . . *brother?*

"Aiden, you idiot!" she hissed, dropping the shard. "What are you *doing* here?"

"Rescuing you!" He sat up woozily, his shaky hand alternately rubbing his bleeding nose and his throbbing crown.

Meg's face flamed bright red. "You're not supposed to be rescuing me! You're supposed to be hundreds of miles from here, looking for a way to help Mom and Dad!"

"Not without you," Aiden said firmly.

"*Yes*, without me. If that's what it takes."

"No," he repeated. "We're in this together. Deal with it."

"I *was* dealing with it!" she stormed. "I was ready to take my lumps for the family. But don't you see? We're *both* trapped now! This place is crawling with police!"

"Yeah, how about that, Meg? You were ready to slice a cop!"

"Not a cop!" She dropped her voice to a whisper. "Hairless Joe."

"Hairless Joe?" Aiden pulled up short. "What's he got to do with anything?"

"He's *here*!"

He stared at her in disbelief. "But — " There

were a dozen reasons why that made no sense at all.

"I just saw him in the parking lot," Meg insisted.

"Hairless Joe? *Our* Hairless Joe? You're positive?"

"I never forget a psycho. He's *tracking* us, Aiden! He must have found out I was with the Brookline police. That's why you shouldn't be here. Now the two of us are in danger!"

"Not for long," Aiden grunted with determination.

"That's easy for you to say. You can just waltz out the way you waltzed in. I'm a prisoner here. My only ticket out is with J. Edgar Giraffe."

He stiffened. "Harris? *He's* coming for you?"

Meg shrugged miserably. "Him or someone just like him. What difference does it make? Either way, I'm not leaving unless it's on the arm of some cop." She frowned at the look of inspired purpose on her brother's face. "What?"

And then she followed his gaze into the closet.

The uniforms! Aiden was going to dress himself up as a police officer and try to march her straight out the front door.

It was brilliant — or possibly very, very stupid. But one thing was clear to Meg. It was their only chance.

She joined him at the closet, searching for a set of dress blues to fit Aiden's slender frame.

"This one feels okay." He pulled the papers of Frank Lindenauer's motor vehicle file out of his pants and stuffed them in the jacket pocket.

"What's that?" Meg asked.

"I'll explain later." He felt around for the buttons and found them on the wrong side. "Wait a minute — this is a *woman's* uniform!"

"It's not my fault you're a beanpole." Meg drew the slacks off the hanger and handed them over. "Hurry up. Hairless Joe could be here any minute."

Aiden scrambled out of his khakis and pulled on the striped trousers. They were a little short, but not obviously so.

Meg fastened the high military collar, pulling it up to conceal his polo shirt. "Nice mustache, incidentally," she told him. "Looks like somebody glued a caterpillar to your face."

He was irritable. "It was more convincing before you put that door through my sinuses. It wasn't meant for soaking up blood."

"Hold still." She got down to her knees and painted his white socks and sneakers with black shoe polish. It wasn't perfect — not by a long shot. But with any luck, nobody would be examining his feet.

"Ready?" Aiden breathed.

She nodded nervously. "Shouldn't I be hand-cuffed or something?"

"Here." He brought her wrists gently together and draped a Brookline PD windbreaker over them. "Stay close to me. And look under arrest."

As they stepped out of the crash pad, Meg glanced back at the piece of paper she had placed on the pillow of the folding cot.

"What's that?" her brother asked.

"Nothing." She closed the door behind them. "Let's go."

19

Aiden marched his sister down the corridor, his face carved from granite. It was an expression he had witnessed on others more times than he cared to remember — the humorless, impassive expression of a policeman escorting a manacled Mom or Dad. After all the Falconer family had been through, the effort of playing captor made him sick.

Too much thinking! he scolded himself. Getting out was all that mattered.

The third floor was still deserted, but the stairs were another story. They passed an officer on the first flight down, and two more on the next. The experience of being looked over by three cops was like an interrogation by enemy spies. But to Aiden's amazement, nobody stopped the escaping siblings. One of the officers even wished Aiden a grunted "Welcome aboard."

He thinks I'm a new recruit!

They reached the ground level and turned down

the central hallway. Okay — barely a football field to go. But it was a teeming, chaotic hundred yards that confronted them. At least eighty people lay between the Falconers and the exit, half of them police personnel.

Meg had never seemed younger — or more terrified. Aiden grimaced from the effort of maintaining his cop face. Ahead lay only peril, but there was no turning back.

They began to walk through the milling crowd. Blue uniforms were all around them, jostling their elbows and shoulders. They did not stop, did not even dare to turn their heads to the left or right. At one moment, the windbreaker slipped from Meg's wrists, revealing that she wore no handcuffs. Aiden shrugged the jacket back into place before anybody noticed.

Fifty yards . . .

No celebration — not yet. *But we're making it. Nobody's giving us a second glance.*

The thought had barely crossed Aiden's mind when someone *did* give them a second glance. In fact, the man stared at them so hard that his eyes nearly shot sparks.

He was in plainclothes like a detective, with a police badge clipped to his shirt pocket.

But this was no detective.

Aiden made the identification in an instant, just as Meg had done. The broad, muscular frame, the shiny bald dome, the ferocious expression . . .

He was looking at Hairless Joe.

He heard Meg gasp, and chomped down hard on the inside of his cheek to contain his own reaction.

The dilemma tore him in two. They had to get away. But the cops would be all over Meg if she tried to run. They were caught — at the mercy of this man who had tracked them from Vermont, who had shot Miguel Reyes, who had already tried to murder them once before.

Immobilized by fate, overpowered by dread, they could only wait for their enemy to attack.

Why doesn't he just do it? Aiden wondered through his agony. *He's got us cornered!*

The answer was obvious: A crowded police station wasn't exactly the best place in the world for a homicide.

He's just as stuck as we are!

The very same cops who threatened the Falconers' freedom were probably also the only reason they were still alive.

Summoning every particle of courage in his exhausted soul, Aiden took another step toward the door. Meg shot him an astounded look but walked along with him. Hairless Joe followed but dared not strike. Anger and malice oozed from every pore on the assassin's bald head. No words passed between them, but the messages of threat and defiance were coming thick and fast, and with impact.

This isn't happening. This is a dream. They were wading through wall-to-wall people, pushing past *cops*. Hairless Joe was three feet behind them. He couldn't make a move on them here, but as soon as they were out in the street, they were fair game. They could fight, but Aiden knew they didn't stand a chance against this killer.

They were beyond the desk now, and the crowd was beginning to thin out. The front door was only twenty feet away. Hairless Joe pushed between an elderly couple to keep pace. His hand brushed against the back of Aiden's police blazer.

Aiden recoiled from the touch as if he'd been splashed with acid. The touch of a man who wanted him dead . . .

If there's a time to run, it's right now!

But Hairless Joe was too close.

What they needed was a head start. Sixty seconds, even thirty. But what could they do without bringing an entire station full of cops down on Meg?

Then it hit him: Use the cops as a weapon.

He shoved Meg toward the exit, spun around, and made a big show of waving both arms in the direction of the enemy. At the top of his lungs he bellowed, *"Gun!!!"*

What happened next was a series of split-second actions. Like compass needles drawn to magnetic north, every officer within earshot wheeled toward the source of the disturbance. A few may have noticed that the stocky bald man was wearing a badge, but most saw a uniformed cop pointing at a noncop, warning that the outsider had a firearm.

Hairless Joe disappeared beneath a barrage of flying blue bodies. Aiden was never sure exactly how many officers flung themselves on top of the bewildered assassin. The instant the ruckus began, he grabbed his sister and hauled her out the door.

They were in full flight along the busy sidewalk, dodging pedestrians and baby carriages. But it was still rush hour. Heavy traffic stopped them at the first intersection.

Meg regarded her brother in pop-eyed respect. "That," she panted, "was the coolest thing I've ever seen!"

Aiden picked his way between idling vehicles.

"Keep moving! Pretty soon they're going to realize Hairless Joe has a badge!"

They scrambled through the cars, ignoring the honking of horns and the curses of frustrated motorists. Trapped in the gap between a taxi and a station wagon, flanked by trucks on both sides, Aiden threw up his hands in frustration. "We're *sorry*!" he bellowed. "Give us a break!"

To his surprise, the horns and shouts ceased abruptly, and the drivers inched forward to clear a path for him.

"Your uniform!" Meg supplied, trailing behind him. "They think you're a cop!"

They hit the sidewalk running. Aiden's chest burned, but he didn't let up, pouring all available energy into the effort to put as much distance as possible between themselves and the police station.

Suddenly, Meg grabbed his arm and squeezed hard enough to splinter bone.

"Aiden," she gasped. "Look!"

20

All Aiden could see was a line of cars pulling out after the green light. "What?"

She pointed. "The red Hummer."

Glaring out over the wheel were the malevolent features of Hairless Joe. The Falconers' head start — their one advantage — had already evaporated.

Aiden gulped. "I didn't think he'd get out of there so fast!"

Meg twirled around frantically. There were no side streets to duck down, no alleys or parking garages. They were hemmed in by the city of Brookline.

Horns sounded as the H-2 cut off the other vehicles and accelerated toward them.

"Let's get out of here!" cried Meg.

But Aiden stepped right out into the path of the speeding Hummer.

"Aiden — what are you doing?"

A freeway exit ramp bottlenecked with the road

just past the intersection. An endless line of vehicles stood there, waiting impatiently to merge. Aiden stuck two fingers in his mouth and emitted an ear-splitting whistle. Moving his other hand in a circular motion, he waved the stopped traffic forward.

"Come on!" his sister urged. "This is no time to play policeman!"

He windmilled his arms, drawing cars onto the street, as the Hummer closed in on him. The rage in Hairless Joe's eyes was visible now. The man understood what Aiden was trying to do and was determined to stop him.

"Aiden — " Meg warned.

Her brother was busy directing a massive tractor trailer onto the road. It was enormous — a semi pulling a fifty-foot flatbed loaded with stacked logs. Its turning radius was too wide, and it lurched to a halt, blocking all four lanes of traffic.

In that awful instant, Aiden realized two things:

1. He had succeeded in shutting down the entire street, and

2. He hadn't left himself enough time to get out of the Hummer's path.

His eyes widened in horror as its cowcatcher screamed toward him at sixty miles per hour.

"Oof!"

Meg hit him in the ribs with a diving tackle worthy of an NFL highlight film. She knocked him backward off his feet and fell over him. They tumbled, somersaulting one on top of the other along the pavement.

Hairless Joe stomped on the brakes, but it was too late. The Hummer slammed into the trailer's steel mass. The front of the H-2 crumpled with a sickening crunch. Steam poured out from under the hood.

The next thing Aiden knew, he and Meg were flat on their backs in the road, and thousand-pound logs were toppling off the damaged transport four feet above them. Without thinking, he clamped his arms around his sister and rolled the two of them under the trailer. There they cowered as a twenty-ton load of wood deposited itself on the streets of Brookline, Massachusetts.

There were cries and shouts and the sounds of car doors as motorists rushed to the spot of the collision. When the booming of falling timber finally ceased, the Falconers scrambled out from under the truck, shaken but, amazingly, unhurt.

Total chaos reigned. Vehicles clogged the roadway around the accident, parked at all angles. Between them were scattered dozens of logs, some of them forty feet long. The driver of the semi was out of the cab, trying to get to Hairless Joe, who was dazed and bleeding into the deflated airbag behind the wheel of the accordioned Hummer. Horns sounded from all directions, a symphony of discord.

"Hey, there's a cop!" a motorist shouted at Aiden. "Call an ambulance!"

The witness later told the police of the inexplicable behavior of the officer on the scene. Instead of offering assistance or calling for backup, the patrolman straightened his crooked mustache and grabbed his companion, a young girl. Without a word to the many onlookers, the two of them fled, sprinting down the road as if pursued by a pack of vicious wolves.

It was almost noon by the time Agent Harris dragged himself up the stairs outside the twelfth precinct house. It was not the flight from Florida that had made him late. What a traffic jam! His taxi had sat at a dead stop for two hours with the meter running while he ran out of coffee, watching a hydraulic crane shuddering under Paul Bunyan–size logs.

Nothing was ever easy where those Falconer kids were concerned.

At least it was done — for Margaret, anyway. Her days as a fugitive were over.

A short, pudgy man with a fuzzy, not-quite-full beard hurried up the steps. He froze when he recognized Harris, whose towering stature made him difficult to miss.

"Agent Harris," greeted Jeffrey Adler, deputy director of the Department of Juvenile Corrections.

Harris skipped the amenities. "Margaret Falconer is not a criminal."

"Tell that to the people she and her brother have robbed this past week," Adler said sharply.

"And we didn't push them to it," Harris retorted. "Sending them to a prison farm."

"Which they burned to the ground," the deputy director reminded him.

"I'll fight you for jurisdiction."

Adler smiled thinly. "That's good. At least you recognize that I'm the one who has it."

Glaring at each other, they entered the building. Harris pressed the advantage of his much longer stride, beating Adler to the desk sergeant. He flashed his badge. "Harris, FBI. I'm here to pick up Margaret Falconer."

The man grimaced. "A little late, aren't you?"

"I hit traffic. Somebody played pickup sticks with a redwood forest out there."

"That's not what I meant," said the sergeant. "The Falconer girl's gone."

"Gone?" repeated Harris. "Gone where? Who with?"

"With her brother, we think. Dressed himself as a cop and walked her right out that door."

Harris's face turned an unhealthy shade of purple. "And you just let them go? Aiden Falconer's a fifteen-year-old kid!"

The man was offended. "Take it easy. We'll get them back."

"You didn't notice when they strolled six feet in front of your desk," Harris growled. "What makes you think you'll find them now?"

"We've put out an APB. In Boston, too."

"It should be all of Massachusetts!" Harris raged. "*And* surrounding states!"

"That's next," the desk sergeant assured him.

"It should be *now*!" He turned, fuming, to Adler. "She's gone."

"Gone? How?"

"Escaped!" Harris's voice dripped with sarcasm. "Prisoners do that sometimes. For some crazy reason, they don't like going to jail!"

Adler faced the desk sergeant. "Are there any leads?"

The man shrugged. "Just the letter."

Harris pounced on this. "She left a letter?"

"But it didn't give us anything we could use. It wasn't really about her."

The FBI agent stared at the Brookline officer. "Then what *was* it about? A thank-you note for your hospitality?"

"She and her brother were holed up at the Royal Bostonian, a posh hotel in the city," he explained. "There have been a lot of high-profile robberies over there. Boston PD didn't have a clue. She put us on to a man using his daughter as a cat burglar. Gave us all the details — that the kid was being forced to steal against her will."

"You mean," Harris was bug-eyed, "that while Margaret Falconer was in this precinct house, in custody, under lock and key — she *solved* a *crime*?"

The man seemed a little miffed. "City cops took all the credit — they grabbed up the dad an hour ago." He smiled slightly. "But — yeah. Nice little piece of detective work. She even supplied the address of the guy who was fencing the goods."

Adler was becoming impatient. "This is all very interesting, but that's *my* prisoner you've allowed to escape."

"And you are?" prompted the desk sergeant.

"Jeffrey Adler. Department of Juvenile Corrections."

The man regarded him in alarm. "You're not Adler!"

"I assure you that I am."

"But he was *here*! He had a badge — Adler from federal Juvenile. He came for the Falconer kid. The whole thing happened right under his nose!"

Harris jumped in. "Describe him."

The desk sergeant shrugged. "Big guy. Bald. You wouldn't believe what those kids did to him."

It was Agent Harris's second nasty shock of the past five minutes. Big guy. Bald. It could only be the mysterious shooter from the summer house in Vermont. Harris had nearly run over the man that rainy night —

Now part of him wished he had.

A feeling of uneasiness took hold in his gut, swelling until it filled the entire six-foot-seven-inch space between the top of his head and the tips of his toes.

The attack in Vermont had been no random occurrence. Someone was after Aiden and Margaret Falconer. Someone besides the FBI, Juvenile Corrections, and several hundred state and local police forces.

Someone with a much darker motive.

But who?

21

Duck Tours were famous in Boston. Their brightly painted vehicles had once been military landing craft, designed to be launched in the water and driven up onto beaches. It was equally common to see these "ducks" driving through city streets or cruising the Charles River, full of sightseers who were encouraged to quack loudly at all passersby.

Two members of the one o'clock trip, however, chose not to join in the fun. They looked enough like tourists, although the teenage boy's pants were striped navy blue slacks, and on closer inspection, his dress shoes were sneakers that had been painted black. He sat with a preteen girl in the last row of the duck, poring over the motor vehicle records of one Francis X. Lindenauer.

"Aunt Jane was right," marveled Meg. "He really was a terrible driver. Look at all those tickets. I'm amazed he didn't lose his license."

"He did," said Aiden in a low voice. "See? Nine years ago. He was driving illegally the whole time he was on vacation with us."

"This is useless," Meg groaned. "I mean, these records tell where he lived around here. But we have no idea where he went after that. Look — this letter was returned with no forwarding address. Are you sure you got all his files?"

Aiden shook his head. "Just the violations part. There were a couple of clerks nosing around. But I'll tell you one thing — no way are we going back to that police station to look for more."

"I hear you," Meg agreed. "If the cops didn't get us, Hairless Joe would. Although," she added, not without a note of satisfaction in her voice, "he's probably out of commission for the next little while."

"It's no joke," Aiden said seriously. "That guy's hunting us, and he's good at it. He's got a fake police badge, and he must have some way to monitor their reports. How else could he know they were holding you in Brookline? We've got a bad enemy, and the worst part is, we don't even know why he's after us. Is he just some wacko who hates our parents? Or is something else going on?"

There was a scattering of quacking and applause as the duck turned off the road, angled down the embankment, and plunged into the Charles. As they hit the water, a blustery wind snatched the documents out of Aiden's hand. The Falconers watched in horror as the vital information took flight over the safety rail and scattered across the river.

They scrambled astern, trying to rescue what they could. Aiden reached for a paper only to have it disappear a split second before he could close his fingers on it. Meg dove for a letter that was hung up on the bar. She clamped her fist around the page, crumpling it into a ball before daring to pull it from the metal.

She turned to her brother. His face — and the dozens of papers littering the Charles — said it all. That file was all they had to lead them to the one man who could save their parents.

Now it was gone, except for the mangled sheet in Meg's hand.

Gingerly, as if handling a piece of thousand-year-old parchment, she unfolded the page. At first she thought it was a piece of windblown litter, since the logo did not match the other correspondence from the city of Brookline and the Commonwealth of

Massachusetts. Then she read the unfamiliar letter-head:

CALIFORNIA DEPARTMENT OF MOTOR VEHICLES

NOTICE OF LICENSE TRANSFER

We acknowledge receipt of the driving record for Francis X. Lindenauer. This license has been converted to California license #6672-787-901. Mr. Lindenauer's current address is 114 Cabrini Court, Apt. 2C, Venice Beach, CA, 90292. . . .

Her hands were shaking, but she kept an iron grip on the letter.

Inches from disaster, and here it was — the clue they'd both been praying for.

Aiden peered over her shoulder. When he spoke, his voice was husky with emotion. He said, "California, here we come."

"California," she repeated. It seemed like the end of the earth. "How are we *ever* going to get there?"

"We'll get there," he said confidently.

The statement was completely illogical. How could they make it all the way to the opposite side of the continent with forty dollars, faces that were becoming more famous every day, and a maniac on the loose who wanted them dead?

Yet somehow Meg knew they *would* get there — just as they'd performed dozens of other miracles since beginning their lives as fugitives.

They would accomplish these things because they *had* to. They had no choice, if they were going to help Mom and Dad.

The duck had conveyed them to the opposite side of the Charles. A few yards away, the grassy river-bank rose into a green, wooded park. A pleasant sign with gold lettering declared WELCOME TO CAM-BRIDGE, MASSACHUSETTS.

She regarded her brother. "Well, it isn't Califor-nia. But at least it isn't Boston anymore."

Aiden nodded decisively. "On three: one . . . two . . . *three*!"

They heaved themselves up and over the safety rail and dropped to the knee-deep water. Meg took her brother's hand, and together they splashed to-ward Cambridge, amid the bewildered stares of their fellow tourists.

By the time the confused shouts got through to the driver of the duck, the fugitives had scrambled up the embankment and disappeared into the cover of the trees.

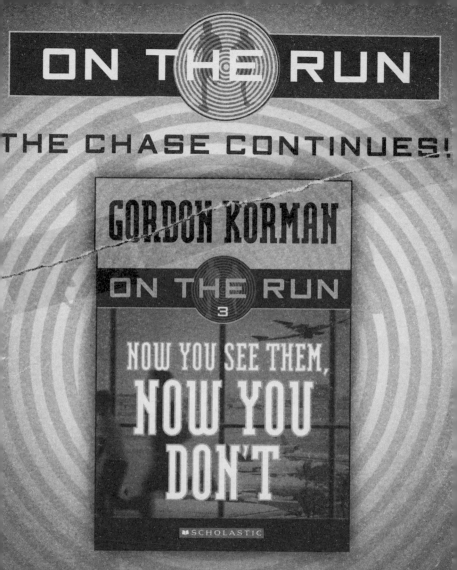

ON THE RUN

THE CHASE CONTINUES!

GORDON KORMAN

ON THE RUN
3

NOW YOU SEE THEM, NOW YOU DON'T

■SCHOLASTIC

...iden and Meg are now the nation's most famous fugitives.
...hey have to work fast to prove their parents' innocence. But
...ere's just one problem—there isn't any proof...yet.

...HOLASTIC and associated logos
trademarks and/or registered
...emarks of Scholastic Inc.

■SCHOLASTIC

OTRBT

EMILY RODDA'S DELTORA

From flying to spying—
choose your adventure!

GUARDIANS *of* GA'HOOLE

Kathryn Lasky

Four orphaned owls band together in this exciting series about an owl world where unknown evil lurks and heroism reigns supreme.

Peter Lerangis

Twins Andrew and Evie navigate a maze of intrigue as they try to uncover the truth about their mother's disappearance in this exciting spy series.